THE LAST
RAINMAKER

Other Books by Sherry Garland

THE LAST RAINMAKER

Sherry Garland

Harcourt Brace & Company

San Diego   New York   London

Library of Congress Cataloging-in-Publication Data
Garland, Sherry.
The last rainmaker/Sherry Garland.
p.   cm.
Summary: Abandoned by her father, thirteen-year-old
Caroline runs away to join Shawnee Sam's Wild West
Extravaganza in the hope of learning more about her
mother, a performer who died in childbirth and whose
origins have been kept a secret from Caroline.
ISBN 0-15-200649-4   ISBN 0-15-200652-4 pb
[1. Runaways—Fiction.   2. Mothers and daughters—
Fiction.   3. Wild west shows—Fiction.   4. Racially
mixed people—Fiction.   5. Indians of North America—
Fiction.]   I. Title.
PZ7.G18415Las   1997
[Fic]—dc20   96-33288

Text set in Granjon
Designed by Lydia D'moch

First edition
F E D C B A
F E D C B A pb
Printed in Hong Kong

To the librarians and good folks
of Nebraska City, Nebraska,
in appreciation of your warm hospitality

Acknowledgments

The list of resources used during the writing of this novel is too great to enumerate here, but I would like to single out just a few books that I found especially helpful: *The Indians of Texas,* by W. W. Newcomb; *Through Indian Eyes,* by the editors of *Reader's Digest; Everyday Life in the 1800s,* by Marc McCutcheon; *Extraordinary Origins of Everyday Things,* by Charles Panati; Don Russell's books about the Wild West and Buffalo Bill; and last, but certainly not least, the several autobiographies written by William Cody (Buffalo Bill) himself.

The old British folk song *Babes in the Woods* is one well-familiar in my family. My mother used to sing it to her children, as I'm sure her mother sang it to her. In fact, an early version, often called *Children in the Woods*, was first printed in sixteenth-century England. Revised many times over, it came to America and existed in many versions, changed to suit American values. For several of those versions, see Vance Randolph's book *Ozark Folk Songs*. The version used in this book is the one sang by my mother as I remember it.

Lastly, this book is a work of fiction. Any similarity of Native American names used in this story to those of real persons, living or dead, is coincidental. Although the famous heroes of the Wild West shows—Buffalo Bill, Pawnee Bill, and Annie Oakley—were the original inspiration for the characters in this novel, Shawnee Sam and Sure Shot Sue are purely fictitious and not intended to reflect the true personalities of those famous persons. In fact, unlike Sure Shot Sue, Annie Oakley was extraordinarily talented, highly respected, and did not have a whiskey-drinking problem.

For further reading about the Wild West era, here are some books that younger readers might enjoy:

L. Alderman, *Annie Oakley and the World of Her Times*

Ingri Mortenson d'Aulaire, *Buffalo Bill*

Jan Gleiter, *Annie Oakley*

Marjorie A. Gurasich, *Red Wagons and White Canvas: Mollie Bailey, Circus Queen of the Southwest*

F. C. Mayers, *The Wild West*

Robert M. Quackenbush, *Who's That Girl with the Gun?: A Story of Annie Oakley*

Stephanie Spinner, *Little Sure Shot: The Story of Annie Oakley*

Prologue

There was a time when Caroline Long believed that life begins when you are born, but that was before she met Billy Big Tree. He taught her that your life really begins a long, long time before your birth. It begins, he said, not with your parents or even your grandparents, but with ancestors so far back that no one remembers their names. He said your life doesn't really have a beginning or an ending—when you're born you're dropped right into the middle of things.

One day Caroline asked Billy Big Tree what he meant by that. Big Tree, as usual, was sitting with his legs crossed, a blanket wrapped around his frail old shoulders to keep out the prairie wind. For a minute or two he stared into the brilliant blue sky, as if he didn't hear the girl. Then he began to speak in that slow, singsong voice Caroline had grown used to.

"I will answer your question with a story," he said.

Caroline had known he would say that, for every time she asked him something important, he would tell her a story or a parable and leave it to her to figure out the answer.

"One day," he began, "a man called Broken Nose rose from his buffalo hide and saw that his pack dog, Short Tail, was not asleep outside his tepee. The dog had a way of wandering off to chase rabbits early in the morning and once had been attacked by a bear; that is why he had only part of a tail. This was the time before the People had been blessed with horses, and a good pack dog was a thing of value. Short Tail was a strong, brave dog, and Broken Nose did not want to train another to take his place.

"Broken Nose walked down the path toward the river, searching for Short Tail. He spied a patch of brown fur fluttering on the mountaintop, and after a long, steep climb he saw that it was not his dog after all but a beaver pelt caught on a bramble under a pine tree. It was a fine day, so Broken Nose sat on the beaver pelt and ate dewberries. While he sat there, he saw a maiden on the side of the slope, picking flowers. He had never seen her before, because she lived in another village on the other side of the mountain. As he watched her, a bumblebee buzzed at her head and when she swatted it she lost her balance and tumbled down the hillside. Broken Nose laughed. She saw him and shouted."

Billy Big Tree grew very quiet.

"Well?" Caroline asked impatiently. "Is that the end of the story?"

"If you want it to be."

"But what happened?"

"I do not know."

"But you were telling me this story."

"The best story does not end. It changes and grows as each man tells it."

"But what was the point of the story? Does Broken Nose marry that maiden?"

"He does, if you want him to."

"Maybe the maiden got mad at Broken Nose for laughing and shot him with an arrow."

"That would be interesting." Big Tree nodded his old head covered with cascading braids of gray hair.

Caroline thought and thought about the story but couldn't figure out how it had anything to do with being born and who your ancestors were. Big Tree didn't say a word; he just puffed his clay pipe—the one that Shawnee Sam had given him years ago. He puffed and Caroline thought.

"I think I know the answer," she said at last. "What really happened was that the dog came out of nowhere and bit the maiden, and she was the chief's daughter so her people went to war with Broken Nose's people and they destroyed each other and that's why there are no Indians on the mountain anymore. But there are a lot of wild dogs, and now they call it Dog Mountain."

Caroline rocked back on her heels, grinning. Billy Big Tree glanced in her direction, puffing on his pipe. Silence filled the air for a long, long, long time. Then he snorted.

Caroline knew then and there that he admired her talents. But it was a long time coming to that point. And if it was true what Billy

Big Tree said about life—that it had no beginning and no end—then Caroline guessed that her own life was a middle. She had always felt that way—that things that had happened before she was born were shaping her destiny, and that things that were happening to her now would shape the destiny of her future children. And since there was nothing she could do about the past or the future, then she guessed she had to make the middle count.

1

It began with the rain, an early spring deluge of undulating gray sheets moving across unplowed fields not yet green with wheat or corn, across dirt roads deep with carriage-wheel ruts, and toward a cemetery on a hill. They shivered that day, a hardy group of mourners standing over a freshly turned grave. But while others shivered from the cold, Caroline Long shivered from the dark, empty place in her chest where her heart should have been.

As a man with unruly red hair wrenched out a melancholy tune on a violin, Caroline felt that her heart—no, her very soul—was being buried alongside her grandmother. The old woman's passing had been sudden and senseless, an accidental drowning in the river that rolled through town. No one had seen her fall in, but they speculated that she lost her footing while walking along a wooden footbridge made slippery from days of rain. As always, Grandmother Long had been on her way to distribute food to the needy, or to sit up with some sick friend. With the thick layers of her petticoats and the yards of dark silk in her skirt, she'd had very little chance of surviving, even if someone had heard her cries for help.

The minister glanced at the approaching rain, then turned his sad eyes to Heaven and swiftly repeated the Lord's Prayer. The mourners said "Amen" with gusto, tossed flowers on top of the casket as it was lowered into the ground, then scattered toward the carriages as the edge of the storm reached the cemetery.

Only Caroline and her great-aunt, Oriona, who was swathed in layers of black, remained at the graveside. Caroline held an umbrella over the old woman while she knelt down to drop a flower on the coffin. Except for the pasty white face half hidden by a black veil, Oriona could have been taken for a pile of black rags rolled into a round bundle. She didn't move, nor did any sound come from her lips. Caroline stepped closer with the umbrella, to better protect her aunt's gray head from the rain.

"Grandmother loved the rain," Caroline said softly. "It seems only fitting that it came to pay its respects, don't you think?"

With great effort and the help of a silver-topped ebony cane, the old woman lifted her rotund body from its kneeling position and turned her pale face toward her great-niece.

"What kind of nonsense are you babbling about now, child? The rain isn't a person; it does not pay its respects."

"I only meant to comfort you, Aunt Oriona. So you wouldn't feel so bad about it raining at Grandmother's funeral. That's all I meant."

"Comfort me! How can you possibly hope to comfort me? I've lost my beloved twin sister. We were born together and we should have died together. Now I have no one left on this earth. My dear husband, my cherished brothers—all destroyed in that wicked War Between the States. My precious babies all taken by the angels. I have no one, no one." The bundle of black shook for several moments, and sobs blended with the sound of wind and rain and distant thunder.

It was easy for Caroline to forget that her grandmother and Aunt Oriona had been twin sisters, for even though their bodies were both round, their facial expressions, manners of dress, and attitudes in general had been opposites. While Onita Long had loved dresses of modern designs in vibrant shades of blues and greens and even an occasional red or pink, her sister, Oriona, had been wearing black since the death of her second husband fifteen years ago. Grandmother Long's blue eyes had twinkled with merriment; Aunt Oriona's pierced like blue icicles. Grandmother Long had taught music at her house on the edge of town, nodding and tapping her toes as her students banged on the piano in the music room. She had loved to entertain, to help those in need, and to attend charity balls. Aunt Oriona preferred to stay at home, sitting beside the window in her black dresses hour after hour, creating lavish needlework projects. She only went out to attend funerals.

Earlier that year when the courthouse clock had struck midnight and the new century had begun, Grandmother Long cheered at the fireworks and waved a tiny American flag along with hundreds of other citizens on the town square. She even played several pieces of rousing patriotic music to welcome the year 1900. Aunt Oriona retired early that night and slept in her bed with a foot warmer.

A rustle of material drew Caroline back to the present. "You have Mattie," Caroline said at last, hoping to cheer her aunt. "Isn't she as good as a daughter to you?"

Aunt Oriona stopped sobbing instantly. She put her gloved hand to her bosom and drew in a sharp breath, as if her niece had mentioned the devil himself.

"Mattie, you say? Hah! My selfish, ungrateful stepdaughter has no more compassion than a stone in the road. She prefers living alone in a miserable boardinghouse in the city to my company. She made her choice years ago, and I'll have nothing more to do with her."

Aunt Oriona set her jaw and through icy blue eyes cast a scathing look at Caroline.

"Why must you insist on stabbing me through with such painful memories in my time of grief? Why am I always surrounded by ingrates and selfish hearts?"

Caroline knew she couldn't console her

aunt, who had broken into more sobs, so she stood by silently, staring at the grave and shivering so hard that her teeth chattered. She watched rain splashing off the weathered tombstones that surrounded them like gray ghosts, those of her grandfather and of Aunt Oriona's two husbands, and the tiny stones of several infants and other long-dead relatives whose lives and loves had been forgotten.

At last Aunt Oriona hushed and jerked the umbrella from Caroline's fingers. With the *tap-tap-tap* of her cane, she labored toward a nearby carriage, where their servant Joshua was trying to calm the restless mule.

"Come along, Caroline. You're getting drenched," Aunt Oriona called over her shoulder as she paused on the stone path. "Your grandmother is in Heaven now. She's not here to indulge your little whims. If you don't come immediately, I shan't allow you in the carriage."

But Caroline lingered a moment longer, her curly black hair plastered to her face, her body shivering uncontrollably as she saw the grave diggers waiting at an appropriate distance for everyone to leave. Her new black dress and high-topped button shoes were getting soaked, and all she had to protect her head was a small black hat with bird feathers made to look like a wing in flight.

Despite the elements, Caroline wanted just a moment more in which to say a final farewell and to wish Grandmother Long a peaceful eternity. It was the first time Caroline had had the chance to be alone with her grandmother since the accident. Even while the body lay in the sitting room receiving visitors for the past two days, it had not been left alone. Teaching piano and violin lessons for thirty-five years had brought Grandmother Long many friends, including former music students and their families. That, and her generous heart and kind disposition.

"Very well," Aunt Oriona said in her crisp, curt voice before she continued to the carriage.

As Joshua helped the ponderous woman into the maroon-colored carriage draped with black sashes, he glanced at the girl on the hill.

"Miss Caroline gon' get soaked to the bone if she don't get in the carriage," he said. "I'd best go take her the umbrella."

"Nonsense, Joshua. Don't pamper that child. She had the opportunity to come with me; now she'll have to walk to the carriage without the umbrella." She poked her head out of the window, and her heavy jowls shook as she shouted in a high-pitched voice, "Caroline, come here!"

In spite of his orders, Joshua dashed to the hill and scooped the girl into his powerful arms. Streams of water spilled over the wide-brimmed hat that he always wore, and his chunky brogan shoes made squishing noises in the puddles. "You shivering like a newborn foal," he said with a grunt. "You gon' catch your death out in this rain."

"I don't want to go back to the house, Joshua," Caroline whispered in a hoarse voice. "It feels all sad and empty without Grand-mother. And Aunt Oriona hates me."

Joshua didn't speak as his arms squeezed tighter. He opened the carriage door to put the girl inside, but Aunt Oriona held up her hand and shook her head.

"I'll not have that wet child ruining my velvet seat cushions. Put her up on the driver's seat with you, Joshua, since you care for her so much." She thrust the umbrella out the window. "You can use this."

Joshua sighed. "Yessum," he said, then placed Caroline gently on the leather driver's seat and climbed up beside her. He removed his waterproof raglan overcoat, the one Grandmother Long had given him, and wrapped it around Caroline's shivering shoulders, then stuck his wide-brimmed leather hat on her head. The water ran off it onto her lap and onto Joshua's waistcoat. Caroline popped open the umbrella and held it above their heads, but even so the rain swept in from the side, chilling them to the bone.

"Yessum, indeed," Joshua muttered. "Wouldn't want to ruin your almighty precious velvet seat cushions what come all the way from Saint Louie." He clucked to the mule, and the carriage jerked forward. The back wheel hit a deep rut, and from inside the carriage Aunt Oriona shrieked. A *rap-tap-tap* sounded on the carriage roof as she poked it with her cane.

"Be careful of those holes, Joshua!" she shouted.

"My, oh, my." Joshua glanced down at the

girl sitting beside him. "Didn't you see that hole, Miss Caroline?"

She looked up into his twinkling black eyes.

"Why, no, Joshua. I surely didn't. Did you?"

"No, ma'am. I surely didn't. And I surely don't see that big ol' hole over there, neither."

Caroline smiled and looped her arm through Joshua's as the carriage bounded from one hole to the next. If it had not been such a sad occasion, she would have come unstitched from laughing by the time they reached the two-story white clapboard house with four gables and dark green shutters. A row of carriages, slicked from the rain, lined the street in front of the house. Caroline dreaded facing the crowd of mourners, but the smoke spiraling up from the chimney reminded her there would be a warm fire waiting inside.

In spite of Joshua's kindness and his attempts to lighten her burden, Caroline's heart could not shrug off the heavy weight pressing on it. Only one thought kept her from bursting into tears as she dashed through the white picket fence's gate and ran between the sculptured evergreens and stately rosebushes swaying in the wind: Immediately after the accident, Aunt Oriona had telegraphed a message to the last known location of Caroline's father, Andrew Jackson Long.

Though she had not seen her father in almost a year, he often wrote letters and sent little mementos of his adventures—a ceramic doll from China, a gold nugget from California, a carved bamboo stick from Mexico. The gloomiest day, the dreariest night, could suddenly turn golden and sunshiney with a letter from her father. After her grandmother's passing, Caroline knew that it was only a matter of time until the man himself, with his twinkling blue eyes and curly blond hair, would appear on the doorstep and carry her away from Aunt Oriona and her black clothes and frowning face. Or better still, he might decide to stay this time, to settle down and live in this little town the rest of his days. And any one of the carriages lined up outside might have brought him.

Caroline dragged her wet, shivering body into the foyer. Already half a dozen greatcoats and several black hats were draped over the rosewood hall tree, and umbrellas filled the slots near its bottom, dripping water all over the ceramic-tiled floor. Some of the men had worn rubber galoshes and discarded them recklessly. Ester would have a fit if she saw the wrought-iron boot scraper on the front stoop with great slabs of brown mud all over it.

Though it was the middle of the day, Ester had already lit the gas wall sconces. They cast eerie golden streaks across the fern in the jardiniere beside the deacon's bench where Caroline sat unbuttoning her muddy shoes. The rain had soaked through her black cotton stockings, making her toes too cold to wiggle. From the sitting room, the sound of many voices mingled with the clink of crystal.

Caroline dreaded going inside, but the warm fire beckoned. As she entered, she saw Joshua's wife, Ester, standing beside the carved marble fireplace, stoking the fire with a poker. Caroline's dark eyes searched the room for signs of her father, but all they found were gray-haired men in stuffy waistcoats hovering near the fire, and gray-haired women sitting delicately on the velvet settee and Louis XV chairs. The heavy damask curtains and mahogany and rosewood furniture kept the room so dark that even the gas chandeliers and the wall sconces could not brighten it. Caroline sighed and stumbled to the beckoning hearth.

At the sight of the shivering girl, Ester dropped the poker and put her hands on her plump hips.

"Why, Miss Caroline, you look worse than that old tomcat what fell into the well last winter. Didn't you use that pretty umbrella ol' Miss Onita bought you last month?"

Before Caroline could answer, Ester grabbed her hands and wrapped them with her own big, warm ones. "Mm, mm, your little hands feel like ice. I suspect your toes feel like icicles right about now, too. I'll boil up some hot water for your foot pan and lay out some dry clothes."

"Ester!" Aunt Oriona called, lowering her body into a lavish wing-back chair with a burgundy cushion trimmed in gold fringe. A heavy sigh escaped her lips. "Before you tend to the child, bring tea to me and my guests. Then lay out my black Henry dress. And boil water for my foot pan, too. I'm afraid I'll catch a fever if I don't get warmed up very soon."

A frown passed over Ester's face, but she

nodded and tore off into the kitchen behind the house. A few minutes later, her daughter, Taffy, who was thirteen years old—the same age as Caroline—came into the room carrying a mother-of-pearl inlaid tray burdened with little fancy cakes, muffins, and other delicacies. Taffy poured steaming tea from an ornately designed silver pot into china cups decorated with pink flowers and distributed them among the guests. Then she filled another cup and handed it to Caroline.

"I'm powerful sorry 'bout your loss, Miss Caroline. Miss Onita was a kindly person. I sure gon' miss her around here." Taffy glanced sideways at Aunt Oriona, then whispered, "Which dress you want me to lay out for you, Miss Caroline?"

"Why don't you choose for me, Taffy? My head is too tired to think right now," Caroline replied.

Taffy loved to rummage though Caroline's things. Sometimes the girls played make-believe and wore each other's clothes. At least they did until Aunt Oriona saw them in the rose garden one day and had a conniption. After a heated discussion, Aunt Oriona convinced her sister that Caroline's clothes might become infested with lice and germs if she let the servant child wear them, so Grandmother Long made the girls stop their game. But sometimes when Aunt Oriona was attending a funeral, which she loved to do, the girls continued exchanging clothes up in the attic. After Taffy had a growth spurt when she turned twelve, she stood a foot taller than Caroline and they looked silly in each other's clothes. But they kept up the game, more to spite Aunt Oriona than for any other reason.

The hot tea warmed Caroline's insides and the hot fire warmed her outsides, but nothing could warm her heart. After a few minutes, she excused herself and climbed the stairs to her room. Everything she saw reminded her of her grandmother, from the black lacquered piano in the music room, to the potted ferns in the sitting room, to the array of ceramic figurines and other bibelots that her grandmother had collected over the years and tucked into glass corner cabinets and displayed on every tabletop available.

In her own bedroom Caroline sat on the dressing-table chair with her feet soaking in a foot pan filled with hot water. Normally she washed or soaked her feet while sitting on a chair in the water closet down the hall, but Taffy was being extra kind to her today. The servant chattered endlessly while she helped Caroline get out of her wet clothes, and while brushing out Caroline's damp hair and re-styling it into a bundle of dark curls, but Caroline hardly heard a word she said.

"Your hair like spun black silk, that's what Mamma say. Even when it get all wet, it still keep its curl. Wish I had hair like yours, Miss Caroline..."

Taffy put the brush down and opened the massive mahogany armoire carved with vines and flowers. "You want to wear your blue dress with the sailor collar, or the red one with the pleats, or this ugly ol' black thing Miss Oriona pull from her hope chest last night?" She removed the selections and laid them across the four-poster bed canopied in white eyelet and lace. The brightly colored dresses contrasted vividly against the white quilted comforter.

"Which do you like, Taffy?"

"If it was me, I bound to pick the red one—that's my favorite. But Miss Oriona, she partial to black all the time. She still wear those widow's weeds after all these years... With your grandmother passing, I suppose you should wear the black one, ugly though it be. With your dark complexion, it gon' make you look like you been in a dust storm. That's what Mamma say when I wear black next to my dark skin."

After Taffy helped her get into the black dress, Caroline stood in front of the floor-length mirror and frowned. Taffy was absolutely right. The dark material made her olive complexion seem even darker and dustier than usual. Caroline jerked it off and put on the red one just as Ester walked past the door. She stopped in her tracks and put her hands on her heavy hips.

"Mm, mm. Miss Oriona gon' bust her corset when she see you in that red hussy dress."

"I don't care. That black one makes me look all dusty. Besides, I want to look cheerful when my father arrives."

"Don't hold your breath 'bout that, chile. That red dress gon' be two sizes too small by the time your father get that message, way over in Californy or Alaska or wherever he be."

"Don't say that," Caroline said, and flung herself on the bed. "Father will be here soon, I know he will. I feel it in my bones."

"You gon' feel something else on your bones, if Miss Oriona catch you in that red dress so soon after your grandmother passed over."

Caroline sniffed and sat up. "Oh, all right. I'll take off the red dress. But I'll not wear that ugly black thing. Grandmother hated black dresses. She whispered behind Aunt Oriona's back all the time about women who excessively wear black. She always said that she wanted to be buried in a blue silk dress. It was her favorite color. Remember?"

"Mm-hm, I surely do."

"Then I'll wear the blue dress, not to spite Aunt Oriona but to please Grandmother. I'll just pretend she is downstairs, waiting to take me in her arms and hug my tears away." Caroline quickly tossed the red dress alongside the black one on the floor. She wiggled into blue cotton stockings, then slipped on the dress with its wide, fashionable sailor's collar and string tie.

As Taffy buttoned it up, Caroline studied the array of framed photographs on the dressing table. The austere, unsmiling faces of her father, Aunt Oriona, Grandmother Long, and Grandfather Long—who had died years before she was born—stared back at her. Even the photograph of Caroline as a baby, swathed in a bundle of white lace, did not smile.

The only smiling face belonged to a woman with black hair and eyes, dressed in a walking-out dress with a high, lacy collar that hugged her neck. But it was not a photograph of Caroline's mother—it was a picture cut out of a *Harper's Bazaar*. Caroline had placed it in a heart-shaped silver filigree frame and pretended that was what her mother looked like. Caroline's mother had died in childbirth, and no one had her picture. All that Caroline knew was that her mother had had dark hair and dark eyes and olive skin. Caroline's grandmother and father said she had been an exotic Italian beauty, descended from a royal family. But more than that, no one would say.

The circumstances surrounding her mother's life and death were the best-kept secret in their house. Caroline had learned over the years that this was a topic that even her kind and generous grandmother would not discuss. But armed with a vivid imagination, Caroline read every bit of information she could muster about Italy, and she collected bibelots from that sunny country until her dressing table and old washstand and every nook and corner dripped with Italian statuettes, fans, pictures, and other knickknacks. She had even learned a few words of the language, of which *bellissimo* was her favorite. She took it to mean "very beautiful" and christened her horse with that name.

The day was miserable and dark. Caroline could see the boarding stable where Bellissimo stayed, not far down the street. She closed her eyes and imagined him prancing around the paddock with the sun glistening on his body, all white except for dark stockings and a dark nose. His highly arched neck and delicately shaped head indicated his fine Arabian bloodlines, and he had a way of not merely trotting but dancing over the ground. Caroline's father had given the horse to his daughter three years ago. There was a rumor that he won Bellissimo in a poker game, but Caroline refused to believe that.

In Caroline's opinion, Bellissimo was the most intelligent horse in town, indeed in the world, and she had taught him several tricks in the past three years. Now she felt restless and sad, knowing that she would not get to see his bright eyes and feel the warmth of his tongue playing with her fingers today. But the rain was falling too hard to go out, and she knew that Bellissimo was locked safely away in the stable. She silently promised that if it did not rain tomorrow she would ride him twice as long and give him a biscuit to make up for her negligence today.

Caroline sat on the dormer window seat, watching the dreary rain, hoping against hope that her father would appear at the door. Taffy tried to cheer her friend with games, but Caroline could not be persuaded to leave her post.

"Miss Caroline, why don't we dig through this ol' trunk Miss Onita left you in her will? I'm dying to peek my nose inside and take a look-see." Taffy dragged in an old Saratoga trunk that had been in Grandmother Long's bedroom for as many years as anyone could remember and that was strictly forbidden to be touched. Many a time the old woman had chastised Taffy or Caroline, or even Ester, for getting too close to it.

Under normal circumstances, Caroline

would have been as curious as any child, but her heart was still heavy. "You go ahead and rummage through it, Taffy. Tell me if you find anything interesting."

Taffy began digging in the old trunk, and soon her excitement turned to disappointment.

"It's just a big ol' pile of nothing," she said. "Her old wedding gown, a bustle, and some other ol' clothes from back before the War Between the States, looks like. Don't know why Miss Onita so secrety 'bout this ol' trunk all the time. I 'spected to see a bucket of gold or rubies and such, from the way she always act."

"What are those bundles of papers?"

"Just ol' love letters. From ol' Mister."

"I guess that's what she was hiding. They're probably full of passion and romantic intrigue."

"Hmmph. Here's an ol' brooch and some other jewelry, but these stones are glass for sure."

"You can have them, Taffy. I'm sure Grandmother wouldn't mind. Anything else?"

"Just a bunch of loose posters, the little kind like you see tacked up on trees and poles when the circus come to town. And looky here, this is the most strange necklace I ever laid eyes on." She held up a massive neckband of tiny beads of red, blue, white, and green. They had been sewn onto a piece of leather to form an intricate pattern.

Caroline took the necklace and turned it over in her hand. She had no idea where it had come from, but it was exotic looking and would fit in nicely with her collection of seashells on the bureau.

"I think I'll keep this one," she said, then looked back out the window.

When the front doorbell jingled, Caroline's heart leaped to her throat. But it was not her father; it was a letter that had arrived in the post. When Ester walked into the room carrying the letter, Caroline immediately recognized the delicate handwriting of her stepcousin, Mattie. As always, it was addressed to Mistress Caroline Elizabeth Long.

Caroline unfolded the letter and pored over the words. Taffy hovered near her shoulder, trying to read. Though she could read and write block letters, she had not yet learned cursive.

As Caroline read, a smile touched her lips. In many ways she hardly knew her older step-cousin, who had run away to Saint Louis five years ago; yet her most pleasant childhood memories centered around this beautiful young woman, who had dared to stand up to her step-mother, Aunt Oriona.

"What do it say?" Taffy asked impatiently. "Is Miss Mattie coming home?"

"It says she has secured a new job as a 'hello-girl.' She works at a switchboard and puts through telephone calls all over Saint Louis."

"Oh, Mamma don't trust them telephones. She say they sound like the devil got your voice, all tinny and small. What else Miss Mattie say?"

"She purchased a pair of roller skates. And she goes bicycling every Saturday. Oh, listen to this, Taffy. She purchased a split skirt so her dress won't get caught in the bicycle spokes. Can you believe that?"

Ester stood in the doorway. "Now don't you go telling Miss Oriona 'bout no split skirt. She have a conniption fit to hear that. What the world coming to, decent young ladies wearing split skirts and riding bicycles? 'Fore you know it, they be wearing knickerbockers and driving motorcars." Ester shook her head and puttered around the room, dusting the figurines.

"That's just what Mattie says, Ester. She rode in an automobile last Saturday. She says it was the most invigorating thing she's ever done and she can't wait for the day when women will have their own vehicles."

"Lawsy, chile!" Ester's eyes grew large. "If you know what's best, you won't tell Miss Oriona one word 'bout none of this newfangled stuff. Now, you wash up for supper. All the guests gone, and Miss Oriona been asking for you."

Caroline sighed. She refolded the letter and put it inside her hope chest along with the stack of other letters, fancy cards, and miscellaneous mementos that Mattie had mailed her over the years. Of all the items, Caroline's favorites were the brightly colored parasols with pictures of flowers or birds or ladies painted on them. Mattie sent a new parasol to Caroline every year for her birthday. It was a little joke between them, for Aunt Oriona and Grandmother Long constantly nagged Caroline never to go outside in the sun without gloves, a hat, and a sun parasol.

"Proper young ladies do not allow the horrid sun to touch their fair skin. With your olive complexion, you'd look like a gypsy," Aunt Oriona would say. Caroline was not even allowed to ride Bellissimo except in the evening, after the sun was low. And while other children played games in the street or in the park, running wild and free, Caroline was allowed only to sit quietly and watch from afar.

Caroline wasn't hungry for supper, but Aunt Oriona insisted she come down and join her at the massive mahogany table with its high-backed chairs and carved ball-and-claw legs. When Aunt Oriona saw that Caroline wasn't wearing black, she promptly sent her back upstairs and chastised Ester and Taffy for not dressing her niece properly for mourning. Caroline would have defied her aunt, except that she did not want Taffy to get into trouble. Besides, by the end of the meal, black suited her mood far better than blue.

The rain had not ceased since the funeral early that afternoon, making the room darker than usual for this time of day. Even the crystal gas chandelier and the burning candles on the dark table could not dispel the gloom. Their golden flames cast eerie shadows across Aunt

Oriona's round face as she ate in silence. Caroline stared out the rain-slicked window, hardly tasting the food or hearing the delicate clink of silver utensils against china. This silence continued throughout the meal, until at last Aunt Oriona patted her lips with a lacy napkin and cleared her throat.

"So...I understand you received a letter from Mattie today. I suppose she's in trouble and needing money."

"No, ma'am. She's got a job as a hello-girl at the telephone company. She makes a decent salary and is doing very well."

"Hmmph. A woman working is scandalous. I don't suppose she'll ever have children now. That's probably for the best, if the father is to be that scoundrel she ran off with. I suppose she is still keeping company with him?"

Caroline took a sip of water from a cut-glass goblet. For the past two years' worth of letters, Mattie had not spoken of the young man she ran off with. The very lack of his mention made Caroline feel sure that he was no longer with Mattie, and likewise made Caroline feel sure that Mattie did not want anyone to know her predicament.

"I'm sure they are doing fine," Caroline

said quickly. "Mattie rode in an automobile last Saturday and said it was invigorating." Caroline decided to take Ester's advice and not mention the roller skates or the split skirt.

"I don't suppose she asked after my health. It wouldn't be like her."

Caroline took another sip of water before answering. "Of course she asked about your health. She says she cares for you deeply and is sorry if she hurt your feelings by running away. She always says that, Aunt Oriona."

Caroline didn't think the little fib would hurt anything. She was so pleased to see Aunt Oriona smile for the first time in days that she took courage and spoke again. "Mattie also expressed her regrets that she couldn't attend Grandmother's funeral. She said she was sorry to hear about it, but she got the telegraph message too late to get here in time."

Aunt Oriona's smile vanished. She slammed her napkin on the plate.

"How dare you lie to me, child! Think of what you're saying. If she did not have time to come to the funeral, then how could her letter have had time to arrive here today? You're a hateful, despicable child to lie to me like that.

I know that thankless stepdaughter of mine cares for no one but herself."

"I only wanted to make you feel better, Aunt Oriona," Caroline whispered, her head hung low.

Aunt Oriona pulled a small fan from her pocket and began swinging it furiously about her flushed face. In a moment she regained her composure and looked at Caroline.

"Now that Onita has passed on," she said, "there will be some changes in this household. My sister was too indulgent with you, just as she was too indulgent with your father, Jackson. Oh, I suppose one might say that since he was her only surviving child, and a son, and the offspring of a dying man, Onita had special reason to spoil Jackson. But I told her again and again that he would break her heart. And that is exactly what he did. Running off and marrying that...that...gypsy."

Caroline lifted her chin and glared at her great-aunt.

"My mother was not a gypsy. She was a well-refined Italian lady with royal blood. I'm proud to have her dark curly hair and dark eyes."

Aunt Oriona snorted. "My dear, you know nothing about your mother, and it will be far better for you if you never do. You may choose to call her a fine Italian lady if you wish, but those of us who were here the night she pounded on the door, on the brink of death, know better. True, you have her dark eyes and dark hair, but the curls came from your father. Your mother's hair was straight and coarse, like a horse's tail."

Aunt Oriona sipped her red wine. A smug little smile crept to her lips, as it always did when she spoke about Caroline's mother. Under normal circumstances, when a similar conversation commenced Caroline would scream back at her great-aunt and stomp her feet. Grandmother Long always took her granddaughter's side. But tonight Caroline's spirits were too low. It was bad enough that her beloved grandmother had been put into the ground that day, but to make matters worse, her father was not there to mourn his own mother's passing.

Caroline did not feel up to arguing about her mother, or her grandmother, or any of the ghosts from the past that Aunt Oriona enjoyed visiting with so much. Caroline sometimes believed that her great-aunt enjoyed carrying on dialogues with the dead more than with the living. Maybe that was why she wore black—because, surely, it was the favored color of ghosts.

Just as Ester was clearing off the dishes, Caroline saw a dark figure pass through the gate of the white picket fence, then heard boots stomping and scraping mud on the front porch. A thrill of hope rushed through her heart and she leaped up, overturning a goblet of wine. The dark liquid spread over the delicately turned lace tablecloth.

"Caroline! Sit back down. Young ladies do not go leaping about when someone rings at the door. Look what you've done to my new tablecloth. It took me months to crochet it." She glared at Caroline with narrowed eyes and tightly clenched lips.

"But surely it is Father," Caroline said, trying to hide the tremor in her voice.

"Nonsense. It's probably another mourner come to pay his respects. Your father no doubt is traipsing around some godforsaken spot of the world and has not even received the telegraph yet. Sit back down and behave yourself."

Caroline poised on the brink of indecision. Part of her wanted to throw caution to the wind and run to the door; another part warned her that such action would only make Aunt Oriona despise her more.

"If you run to the door, you shall be punished severely," Oriona admonished. "I am in charge of this house now, and there shall be no running and acting like a savage." She rapped the floor with the silver-topped cane to emphasize her words.

Without delay, Caroline spun on her heels and ran to the foyer, bumping into a potted palm in her haste. She pushed poor Ester aside and grabbed the cut-glass knob. Her heart pounded in her chest as she flung open the door.

2

"Father!" Caroline shrieked, and threw her arms around the waist of the tall, broad-shouldered man with wavy blond hair. His long overcoat dripped with rainwater, but she didn't care. Suddenly the cold lump in her chest melted away, and nothing Aunt Oriona said or did could ruin the night. Her father was here to take her away from her aunt's cold eyes and bitter heart and hovering ghosts.

Jackson Long's body shook with sobs for a moment as he hugged his daughter. Caroline breathed in the smells of tobacco and wine and dust and horses and leather—the smells of her father.

Jackson released Caroline and sat on the

deacon's bench. She removed his muddy galoshes to expose shiny brown shoes with white spats buttoning up the sides. Ester helped him out of his wet raglan coat and brown homburg hat, then hung them on the hall tree. Before entering the sitting room, Jackson took a quick look at his reflection in the hall mirror and adjusted his paisley waistcoat, large knotted tie, and stiff white butterfly collar. Caroline proudly looked at the handsome features. Surely there was no other man on earth as dashing as her father, she thought as they walked into the sitting room arm-in-arm.

Jackson positioned himself on the settee nearest the fire, carefully arranging the crease in his pants. As he held his hands out for warmth, Caroline scooted beside him as close as possible.

"Did you see Grandmother's grave?" Caroline asked in a quavery voice.

Jackson nodded. "That's why my galoshes are so muddy. I'm sorry I missed Mother's funeral." Tears filled his intense blue eyes and rolled down his cheeks into his large blond mustache. "I came as soon as I got the telegraph message." He wiped his tears away with his thumb.

"Were you in the Yukon prospecting for gold, Father? Did you have to fight off grizzly bears and a pack of wolves?"

He laughed and squeezed Caroline's hands. "No, sweetest, all the good gold claims have already been taken. Alaska is a madhouse full of ruffians and ne'er-do-wells. And no place for a gentleman. Actually, when the telegraph message caught up with me I was on a steamboat coming up from New Orleans. I was already halfway here or I shouldn't have been able to return home so fast. I'm investigating a new enterprise down south. A fabulous land speculation. If this project comes about, you and I shall be so rich we'll leave behind this dreary little Missouri river town and travel around the world to the most exotic places you've ever dreamed of."

"What places, Father?"

"The Orient, jolly old London, gay Paree, the jungles of Africa, the Pyramids of Egypt. How would you like to ride up the Nile?"

Caroline's pulse raced at the prospect of going anyplace with her father. It really didn't matter where. In fact, what she truly wished, more than anything, was that he would settle down in this dreary little river town, in a house with a rose garden out front. But her grandmother had often said that Jackson had wandering feet, so Caroline would be happy to travel the world, if that was what it took to be with him.

"A trip up the Nile would be splendid, Father. And so would a trip to Italy. Perhaps we could find some of Mother's relatives there. Do you know in which city she was born?"

As he always did whenever Caroline mentioned Italy or her mother's people, Jackson grew evasive and quickly changed the subject.

"Stand up a moment so I can see you more thoroughly."

Caroline stood and turned around twice, wishing that Aunt Oriona had not made her change into the dull black dress she now wore.

"You've grown so, I hardly know you anymore. Soon you shall be swept off your feet by some dashing young man and you'll forget your dear old father."

Caroline shook her head and crawled back onto the settee and looped her arm through her father's.

"I shall never, never forget you, Father. Even when I am old and wrinkled and gray and walk with a cane, I shall remember you." She traced her finger over his thick handlebar mustache, then pressed the dent in his chin, which felt all prickly with whisker stubble. "When I grow up, I hope I marry a man exactly like you."

"Now, that would be another mistake for this family." Aunt Oriona's voice crackled in the air as she tapped her way into the sitting room. The layers of petticoats and silk hissed as she walked by.

Jackson loosened his daughter's grip and stood up.

"Good evening, Aunt Oriona," he said, bowing at the waist. He took her elbow and assisted her to her favorite wing-back chair with its plush-cushioned seat of gold brocade and black velvet. "You're in good health, I pray."

She waved him away with a pale hand. "I'm sure my health is of little concern to you, Jackson. I must say I am surprised to see you so soon. You must have been closer at hand than everyone thought."

Ester slipped into the room and placed the

silver tea service on the gold-leaf occasional table in front of the settee. Jackson poured a cup and took a sip of the hot liquid before responding to his aunt's comments.

"Actually, I was already on my way home to visit Mother and, of course, Caroline when your message caught up with me. I was on a steamboat. Luckily I had told friends in New Orleans my plans and they got the message to me ... If I had only arrived a few days earlier, Mother would be alive now, I know. Oh, the irony of my mother dying in the river that she loved so dearly!" He slumped back down onto the settee and hung his head in his hands.

Caroline stroked his soft blond curls.

"Poor Father. You just missed seeing Grandmother. She would have been so happy to see you."

Aunt Oriona snorted rudely. She picked up her embroidery hoop and slid on a pair of reading glasses, then moved the parlor lamp closer.

"There's one reason and one reason only that you ever return home, Jackson. You ran out of money and were coming to borrow more from Onita." She began pulling the needle and thread through the cloth, her plump fingers amazingly delicate and agile as they followed the pattern of a bouquet of yellow daffodils.

"That isn't true!" Jackson leaped to his feet. He ran his fingers through his hair and began pacing in front of the fireplace. "I loved Mother, and I love Caroline."

"No doubt you do. But you love adventure and worthless schemes even more. What doomed investment did you intend to throw Onita's money after this time?"

Caroline couldn't bear another moment of her great-aunt's insolent tone. She grabbed her father's hand and pressed it to her face.

"It isn't a doomed investment," she said. "Father has great plans for a land speculation deal that will make us enormously wealthy. We're going to travel the world together." She thrust her chin out and glared defiantly at Aunt Oriona, whose fingers did not even pause in their work and whose eyes did not look up.

"I see," Aunt Oriona said. "And I suppose you expected Onita to give you the last of her available money?"

"No! I never expected her to *give* me money, only to lend it. I would have invested it and repaid her tenfold. This land deal cannot go wrong. I would have made Mother wealthy beyond her wildest dreams." He paused, then broke free of his daughter's hands and stood in front of Aunt Oriona. "What did you mean when you said 'the last' of Mother's money? She had abundant funds the last time I communicated with her."

"I said 'available' money. After she changed her will, her available funds were not as abundant as you might think."

"She changed her will? When?"

Aunt Oriona didn't respond for a moment, and Caroline grew impatient to hear her reply. Even Joshua, Ester, and Taffy were lingering in the hallway just outside the sitting room door.

Aunt Oriona basked in the attention and in the power she held over them all. Meticulously she pulled the thread and needle, engrossed in a tiny cross-stitch leaf. At last her nephew lost all patience and ripped the hoop from her hands.

"What did she change in her will?" he demanded.

"It took her the past thirteen years, but at last Onita came to her senses and regained reason. At last she realized how you had squandered her money on one foolish scheme after another—gold nuggets in Alaska, china figurines from the Orient, hotels in Mexico, gambling debts at every turn. Oh, the list is endless. And your association with that—that gypsy woman."

"Leave the dead out of this conversation, Aunt Oriona."

"I told Onita you were a spoiled, thankless child who should have been looking after his widowed mother and his motherless child all these years instead of running from responsibility at every turn. If it hadn't been for your father's wise investments during the War Between the States, and my second husband's help with the business, there would not have been a penny in this household."

"You old biddy! What bitter poison did you put in Mother's heart to make her turn against her only son, who loved her dearly?"

"You had a strange way of showing your love, Jackson, never being home except when you needed more funds. All I did was point out the truth; it was your actions alone that made her rewrite her will. She knew that poor

Caroline would end up a penniless orphan if she did not."

"How much did she leave me, then? Only half?"

Aunt Oriona shook her head gravely.

"One-third? Oh, cruel fate to have one's own mother betray you!" Jackson swiped a tea-cup off the tray. The delicate white-and-pink china crashed against the marble hearth.

"You would be fortunate indeed to have received that much, considering your thoughtless ways," Aunt Oriona said calmly.

"Less than one-third? That is not possible."

Aunt Oriona picked up her needlework from the floor and looked directly at Jackson. A glowing light passed over her face.

"Dear, dear nephew. Onita came to her senses just a few days before her untimely death. She cut you out of her will. Do you hear me—she cut you out entirely." She rapped her cane as she spoke.

The color drained from Jackson's face, and he dropped to his knees across from the chair where Caroline sat. His body trembled with anger, and when he spoke, it was through clenched teeth.

"And what about Caroline? Mother loved her like her own daughter. Surely this innocent child was not disowned, too?"

"Of course not. Onita left the bulk of the estate to Caroline and the rest to me."

Jackson sighed and held his arms out for his daughter. Caroline slid into them, still stunned by all she had heard. She had no idea how much money her grandmother had possessed. It was not polite for women to discuss financial matters. And though she did not consider her family wealthy, they never lacked for anything unless it was an extravagant luxury, like an automobile.

"It will be all right, Father," Caroline said, and stroked his furrowed brow. "I don't want Grandmother's horrid old money. I shall give you every penny I inherit."

Jackson drew his daughter closer and kissed her cheek. "Sweet angel, you are too good to your undeserving father." He stood up, taking Caroline's hand. "There, you see, Aunt Oriona, all your bitter scheming was to no avail. My beautiful child has a generous heart."

"Ah yes, Caroline's generous heart is renowned. That is precisely why your mother put all of the child's inheritance into a trust fund. Caroline will not be able to touch it until she is eighteen, nor will you. In the meantime, I am trustee of her funds and shall spend them as I see fit for clothes and other necessities. Even you cannot get your hands on the money, at least for five years. And believe me, not an extra penny will Caroline be allowed to pass on to you. If she misbehaves, she won't receive a nickel." With finality in her voice, Aunt Oriona rose and began walking to the stairs.

"You beastly old shrew!" Jackson hissed at her back, then spun on his heel.

"Joshua!" he shouted. "Hail me a hackney. Ester, bring my coat. I'll not stay another minute in this house."

"Father!" Caroline clung to his hands, but he brushed her aside.

"Not now, Caroline. I'm in no mood to be pleasant."

"Where are you going?"

"I don't know, but I refuse to stay the night where I am so unwelcome. My own house! I am being removed from my own house! You'll not get away with it, you old crow!" he shouted at Aunt Oriona as she lumbered up the stairs.

"I swear by my mother's grave I shall go to a solicitor and find a way to get my rightful inheritance. And I'll take the house and business and everything else, and boot you out."

Aunt Oriona paused on the landing in front of a floor-length rosewood mirror, making it appear that two Aunt Orionas breathed heavily and clasped the banister.

"Onita's will was properly prepared by the best solicitor in town and is binding. And besides, you haven't the funds to hire a lawyer. Good night, Jackson, and good-bye."

From the way her father gripped the banister, Caroline thought he was going to rush up the stairs and push Aunt Oriona off the landing. But he controlled himself in a manly way and quickly put on his galoshes, coat, and hat. Caroline ran to him and seized his hand.

"Father, please take me with you."

"I have no place to stay, child. I'll most likely sleep in the barn tonight with your horse, and have to share his oats on top of that."

"I don't care where I sleep, Father. Please, please don't leave me here with Aunt Oriona. She hates me. You heard her—she is going to put reins on me like a mule and tell me what to do all the time. I would rather be a pauper with you than stay here with her. Please, Father." Tears rolled down Caroline's cheeks.

For a moment Jackson stared at the empty staircase. Then a smile crept to his lips. "I have an idea, sweet one. But I need to consult with the solicitor before I act. Stay here tonight, and I swear by my mother's grave that I will return in the morning to get you. Pack your clothes and precious things, but do not tell your great-aunt what you are doing. If all goes as I hope, you will never set foot in this miserable house again." He kissed his daughter's cheek, then adjusted his homburg and ran into the rain. Caroline watched him climb into a cab and heard a whip crack.

Upstairs in her room, Caroline called Taffy and Ester in to help her pack and swore them to secrecy. They didn't know what to think, but they did not blame Caroline for wanting to get away from Aunt Oriona.

Caroline gave Taffy all the dresses she could not fit into two Saratoga trunks—one being the old trunk that her grandmother had given her. She gave all her toys to Ester's two youngest children and gave her beautiful doll-house with gabled roof and little white gazebo to Taffy. The gilded birdcage and cheerful yellow canary she instructed Ester to give to Joshua, who had long admired its lovely singing.

"I sure gon' miss you, Miss Caroline," Ester said as she folded Caroline's favorite white cotton petticoat.

"Wish you didn't have to go away," Taffy added, fighting back the tears.

"How I wish I could stay, too, but Aunt Oriona hates me."

"Oh, I 'spect it ain't you she hate so much as what you remind her of," Ester said.

"What do you mean, Ester?"

"Miss Oriona couldn't have no chile. All her babies died when she was young. Then her first husband, the late colonel, gone and got hisself kilt in the War Between the States. She married again, but the doctor say Miss Oriona too messed up on the inside to have another chile, so her second husband play around with the ladies a lot. He got hisself shot down by the river docks 'cause of some hussy gal. Miss Oriona been 'bout the bitterest woman I ever seen all these years. Wearing black and harboring hatred and jealousy for her own sister."

"But Grandmother had bad luck, too.

Grandfather died in the same war, didn't he?"

"Ol' Mister, he died 'cause of that war, but not in it. He got hisself wounded severely, but he come home after it end. He linger on two whole years before dying from his wounds, but that was long enough for him to sire a son what wasn't born till after Ol' Mister cold in the ground. Miss Onita, her first two babies died, too, and everyone suspect the same of this one. But Andrew Jackson, he strong and healthy. Everybody say he a miracle baby and no wonder Miss Onita dote on Andrew Jackson. But Miss Oriona, she don't never forgive her sister for having a chile that live and for having a little bit of happiness.

"I think Miss Oriona be glad when Andrew Jackson run off one summer and work in the Wild West show in Saint Louie. The sadder Miss Onita get, the happier Miss Oriona get. Then when you got borned and brought some sunshine into this dreary old house, Miss Oriona really be full of bitterness. I think she almost glad your grandmother die, just so she could kick Andrew Jackson out and make your life miserable and drive you away.

"Just like she drive poor Miss Mattie away.

That po', po' chile never got one kind word from Miss Oriona. Miss Oriona hate her step-daughter 'cause she young and pretty and have plenty of beaux lined up in the parlor. Miss Mattie run away with that slick no-'count Philadelphy lawyer and hain't step foot back in this house since."

All the while Ester talked, Caroline packed a leather portmanteau with shoes and stockings and filled a small carpetbag with items from her dressing table—combs, brushes, perfume bottles, embroidered handkerchiefs, and pictures. She stopped when she reached the heart-shaped silver frame containing the picture of the Italian lady. Caroline's finger gently traced the curve of the beautiful face.

"Ester, did you know my mother?" she asked.

Ester shook her head. "No, missy. Didn't nobody meet your mama till the night she show up on the door stoop, fixing to birth her baby. She had long black hair and big black eyes and a dark complexion, but it be late at night and only one little lamp burning in the room. Couldn't see much. She spoke in some foreign tongue, couldn't nobody understand what she say, and po' Jackson was still a chile hisself, being only nineteen years old and way too young to become a papa. The whole thing just about broke his heart in two."

Caroline slipped the small picture frame into her dress pocket. She didn't need to hear the rest of the story. Her grandmother had told her often that her mother died just after the baby was born, and Jackson, torn with grief, left to make his fortune in the western territories. But Caroline never once doubted that her father loved her. He came home at least once a year, usually at Christmas, and wrote letters and sent little souvenirs. She would not trade him for any other father alive, except maybe to make him settle down a little. But none of that mattered now. In the morning her father would take her away from Aunt Oriona and her bitterness.

Rather than putting on her muslin nightdress to prepare for bed, Caroline changed into her favorite blue dress with the white sailor collar and matching blue cotton stockings. She was determined to stay awake all night, in case her father appeared suddenly. Taffy tried to stay up with her friend, but her eyelids grew heavy and she fell asleep just past midnight.

The house grew eerily silent, disturbed only by Taffy's slow, even breathing and the loud ticking of the grandfather clock in the foyer. Caroline tiptoed downstairs and in the darkness wandered from room to room, touching furniture and vases and knickknacks that she had grown up with and that her grandmother had cherished. The kitchen still smelled of spices and tea, and the great chopping table was covered with pies and cakes brought over for her grandmother's wake. Enough to feed Coxey's army, her grandmother would have said. The ice had almost melted in the wooden icebox, but the milk was still cool and pleasant enough to drink with a piece of chocolate cake.

After eating, Caroline slipped into the water closet—or as her grandmother called it, the necessary room. It was the most recent addition to the house, being finished only a week ago. The ceramic bathtub sat at one end of the room on stately claw-foot legs, and the brass fixtures were shaped like dolphins to complement the washbasin, which rested on the shoulders of a pedestal dolphin. A settee, a potted fern, an oval mirror flanked by scalloped gaslights, a bamboo towel stand, and a chair to rest in while having a footbath made it the most modern room in the old house. The former water closet had been just that, no more than a small closet with a toilet, tucked away in a corner of the hall.

How Caroline's grandmother had fussed with the carpenters, and purchased each fixture and motif only after great forethought, selecting and discarding the wallpaper pattern five times before deciding on the pale salmon seashells on a soft green background. She had pulled the cord handle on the high-hanging wooden water tank again and again to test its power, while Ester and Taffy had squealed in delight as the water swirled in the toilet bowl.

"It's 1900! We must keep up with the times," Grandmother Long had said with a cheery smile when she first started the project. Now the dear woman would not get to enjoy her precious necessary room or show it to party guests at Christmas, or to her music students and their families at recitals.

After washing her hands, Caroline slowly climbed the stairs to her bedroom. Taffy still slept soundly on the chaise longue, her arms folded across her chest. Caroline draped a bright patchwork quilt over her friend, then sat at the window seat and looked down at the rain-slicked street. Though it was no longer raining, swirling fog had rolled in, haloing each gas streetlight with eerie colors. Not a single carriage nor pedestrian could be seen, and the dogs didn't even bark.

Caroline shivered and pulled her fringed cashmere shawl around her shoulders. She removed the heart-shaped picture frame from her pocket and studied the Italian woman's face. As always when she studied the picture, Caroline wondered how different her life would have been with a mother. A mother to love and care for her, to teach her how to sew and cross-stitch and dance and all the things a girl needed to know. A mother to help her select party dresses and teach her how to play croquet on the lawn and how to handle annoying boys with bugs and worms in their fingers. Most of all, a mother to share her fears and dreams with, to hold her tight on rainy, stormy nights.

Caroline wondered if her mother would have approved of all the newfangled inventions like bicycles and roller skates; would she have been old-fashioned and strict, like Aunt Oriona? Surely her mother would have ridden in an automobile. After all, she had performed in a Wild West show.

The only thing Grandmother Long claimed to know was that Caroline's mother had ridden a trick horse, a beautiful white horse so intelligent that it could dance. Sometimes, when riding Bellissimo, Caroline pretended that she, too, was in a Wild West show.

When the grandfather clock bonged three times, Caroline could not fight sleep any longer and closed her weary eyes. She dreamed of her mother, her long black hair flying in the wind as she rode on the back of a dancing white horse. And Caroline rode beside her.

Caroline awoke to the sound of a loud commotion on the staircase. Peeking out the bedroom door with Taffy, she saw her father and Aunt Oriona climbing the stairs, screaming and shouting at each other. At last her father had come to rescue her from Aunt Oriona's biting tongue. Caroline did not know where her father would take her, or how they would live, but it did not matter as long as they were together.

3

Caroline's head felt groggy from lack of sleep and the early hour. Amidst the shouting and confusion, Jackson charged the stairs and grabbed his daughter's hand. Never had she seen his face so full of fury; his blue eyes glowed and his cheeks were flushed crimson. Aunt Oriona lumbered up the stairs, stopping to catch her breath at the landing and clutching her heaving bosom.

"You shan't get away with this, Andrew Jackson Long," she cried in a piercing voice. "This is child nabbing. I'll have the constable after you before you reach the river."

But Jackson refused to speak, except to bark orders at Joshua and Ester to carry down Caroline's luggage. Ester scurried about, torn between obeying Jackson and heeding Aunt Oriona's counterorders. When Joshua hesitated, Jackson threw open a window and shouted down at the cab driver to come up and help with the trunks.

Taffy wept and clung to her friend's hand all the way down the stairs. Then Ester's two youngest children, awakened by the commotion, began crying and tugging at her skirts, adding to the confusion until Caroline felt she was in the midst of a P. T. Barnum circus ring.

When Caroline stepped out the front door, she saw a hansom cab parked in the drive. To her amazement, her horse, Bellissimo, was tethered to the back of the carriage, wearing his beautiful European saddle. Happiness raced through Caroline's heart. She was sure she could not have parted with her beautiful horse, and she loved her father more than ever for such thoughtfulness.

Just as the hall clock bonged seven times, the front door burst open and her father came out.

"Come, Caroline," Jackson said as he adjusted his homburg hat. "We've no more reason to stay in this house." He seized her hand and ripped her away from Taffy.

"Driver, are my daughter's belongings secured?"

"Yessir," the cabby replied.

"Then we're off." He opened the carriage door and helped his daughter climb onto the step board. As she scooted over to make room for her father, Caroline smelled the worn leather of the seats and the lingering scent of tobacco and perfume from previous passengers.

Caroline drew back the carriage curtains and looked out the window. Aunt Oriona wasn't crying, but her usually pale face was rosy pink and her chest heaved. No doubt she would suffer from a case of the vapors and send for the physician before the hour was up.

Ester and Taffy wept openly. Even Joshua's merry eyes looked sad as he held his hat in his hand and waved slowly with long, bony fingers. Caroline would miss them tremendously. Taffy was more like a sister to her than a servant, as they had been raised side-by-side for the past thirteen years. Only the knowledge that she was about to begin a life of adventure with her father kept Caroline's tears from falling, too.

The horses' hooves clopped on the brick pavement, echoing in the cool morning air, and soon the carriage fell into a gentle rocking motion. There was very little traffic, and the thick fog gave a feeling of eerie isolation.

Though Caroline had a thousand questions for her father, her instincts told her not to speak until he had calmed down. His tight lips and clenched jaw warned that he was in no mood for idle conversation. Caroline was sad to be leaving the only home she had ever known, yet at the same time she was fulfilling a lifelong dream—to travel and live with her father.

Caroline was sure their destination was the river, with its steamboats and bustling docks. She imagined they would return to New Orleans, stay in the French Quarter, stroll the gardens, and see the sights before deciding where to travel. She had never been out of this little river town more than a few miles, for Sunday excursions in the summertime; and the thought of taking a long trip down the Missouri and the Mississippi thrilled her.

The heavy fog prevented her from seeing the street signs, and more than once the cabbie missed a turn and had to backtrack his route. When the carriage finally stopped and Caroline stepped down, she saw not the busy river docks, alive with stevedores loading bales of cotton and barrels of whiskey and molasses onto barges, but rather the train station.

While the cabdriver untied the trunks and her father walked to the ticket office, Caroline stroked Bellissimo's smooth white face and soft muzzle.

"I'm so glad you are coming with us, Bellissimo," she whispered. "I don't think I could live without you. I don't know where we are going, but shan't we have fun riding together on this adventure? Maybe we shall go out west and see cowboys and Indians. Or perhaps we'll go to some tropical island and you can drink coconut milk all day." The horse whinnied softly and shoved his muzzle into Caroline's chest.

All around her, wagons creaked with their loads of cotton, farm tools, and barrels that had been unloaded from the boats yesterday. These goods would go by train into the interior of America, to cities in the Midwest and beyond. Most of the passengers were businessmen, from the looks of their dark morning coats and their black bow ties worn over stiff collars and boiled shirts.

After a few moments, Jackson stepped out

of the ticket office, engaged in a lively conversation with a stranger dressed in a sporty Norfolk jacket, knickerbockers, and knee-high gaiters, as if he had just come from a day of hunting.

The cabbie placed Caroline's trunks and leather portmanteau on the wooden platform. From there a baggage handler loaded the belongings onto the train with such a lack of concern that Caroline was sure that everything inside would be broken into little shards. She kept with her the small carpetbag with a few personal items, and her favorite crocheted handbag.

The engine hissed and steam rolled from under its black body, then a sharp whistle pierced the air. The conductor bellowed, "All aboard!" and people said their final good-byes.

"Where is this train going, Father?" Caroline asked.

"Saint Louis," her father replied as he removed a piece of thick paper from his pocket. "Here is your ticket, Caroline. Don't misplace it."

Caroline gawked at the ticket. It had names of many small cities on it, but the final destination was Saint Louis, Missouri. She had never been there but, of course, Mattie had told her many wonderful stories about its beauty and its fascinating people. It was not as exciting as Alaska or China, but Caroline would be happy anywhere with her father. She smiled.

"So we are moving to Saint Louis? I hear it is a grand city."

Jackson glanced at the stranger in the Norfolk jacket, then put his hand on Caroline's back and guided her to the steps of the passenger car.

"Get aboard, Caroline. The porter will take care of all your needs. Here's all the money I can spare." He dropped a small leather pouch of jingling coins into her hand. "Guard it carefully and do not let anyone talk you into spending it foolishly. My stepcousin, Mattie Rowe, will be waiting for you at the station in Saint Louis."

"Cousin Mattie! That's wonderful. But wait—you speak as though you aren't coming, Father." Suddenly Caroline's stomach felt queasy. Panic raced through her heart and her pulse quickened.

A sigh escaped from Jackson's lips and

Caroline knew before he spoke that her worst fears were founded. Her father was not taking her to New Orleans or any other place. Tears blurred her vision, and she blinked furiously.

"You promised me, Father. You said we would travel the world together—China, Italy, Africa. Remember what you said?"

Jackson took her hands. "I want to, I truly do, but you are too young to go on adventures. I know nothing about caring for a child. The world is too dangerous for you."

"Then why did you take me away from Aunt Oriona? Why did you pretend that you cared about my future?" Caroline ripped her hands from his.

"Because that old shrew only wanted you around so she could collect money from your trust fund. With you gone, she will not be able to get her hands on a single penny."

"And what about me, Father? Am I to live like a pauper?"

"Cousin Mattie will take good care of you until I am back on my feet and can come get you. It won't be so long, only a few weeks. I'll write you often. Just think, when you turn eighteen you'll be old enough to travel with me all over the world."

"And rich enough to support you!...Oh, Aunt Oriona was right, wasn't she? You only came to visit Grandmother when you needed money, and not to see me!"

Jackson remained silent a moment, then adjusted his hat.

"I hope that someday you come to understand that I'm thinking of what's best for you. Remember, no matter what your aunt says, I do love you." He pulled her close and buried his face in her neck a moment, then kissed her cheek. "Good-bye, my darling Caroline. Please forgive your old father."

"Go away." She choked on the words and pushed him back.

He looked at her a long time, then cleared his throat.

"There's one more thing," he said cautiously. "I'm taking your little horse with me."

"Bellissimo! Why?"

"I've just spent the last of my money for your train ticket. At least with a horse, I can ride back to New Orleans. Anyway, there's no place for him to stay at Cousin Mattie's board-inghouse."

Caroline saw the stranger in the Norfolk jacket walking around Bellissimo, stroking its silvery neck.

The truth struck her with the force of light-ning. "You're going to sell Bellissimo! I hate you, Father. I hate you!" With a surge of anger, Caroline turned and ran up the steps, ignoring her father's shouts.

She followed the porter to the booth as-signed to her in the so-called ladies' car, which in spite of its name contained several men who were smoking cigars and chewing tobacco without regard to the requests of the women. Caroline settled into a seat next to a window.

Her shattered heart told her not to look outside, but she did. She saw the stranger in the Norfolk jacket swing up onto Bellissimo, then ride him in a circle. After dismounting, he counted out a bundle of money and put it in Jackson's outstretched hand. As she watched the stranger climb back onto Bellissimo and ride him down the street, Caroline could not fight back her tears any longer. Her father stood beside the hansom cab, watching the train slowly pull away. He held his hand up, and his blue eyes glistened with sadness, but Caroline turned her back on him.

The bitter gall of betrayal stayed fresh in Caroline's mouth for the rest of the long, arduous train trip. The loudness of the wheels against the metal rails, the stench of the burning coal, the disgusting tobacco being spit all around her, in and near spittoons, made Caroline's stomach turn. She lost all appetite and didn't go to the dining car but rather nibbled on some peanuts and a day-old sandwich peddled by the train butch.

No one met Caroline at the station, and she had to hire a hackney to take her to the modest boardinghouse where Mattie Rowe lived. The old two-story house, run by a stout, redheaded widow named Mrs. Carraway, was popping at the seams with boarders and seven little redheaded, freckle-faced Carraway children.

When Mattie finally arrived, she smothered Caroline with kisses and hugs. Caroline had remembered Mattie as a young woman prone to wearing dull-colored dresses and an unflattering hairstyle much like Aunt Oriona's. How she had changed! Her chestnut hair was now swooped up in a soft, fluffy style, topped by a bright wide-brimmed straw hat crested with wax flowers. Her brilliant yellow blouse with navy polka dots had leg-of-mutton sleeves puffed out at the shoulders but narrowed tightly around the forearm and wrist. Her high-topped laced shoes peeked from beneath a navy blue skirt that didn't quite touch the ground. Her wide leather belt had a small silver buckle in the shape of a hand holding the prongs in place. But most wondrous of all, over her shoulder she'd slung a pair of roller skates!

"I'm sorry I didn't meet you at the station," Mattie said, out of breath. "I thought I would be back in time, but Albert insisted on another tour around the roller rink."

Caroline took the skates in her hands and smelled the leather. A warm feeling came over her as she looked up into her cousin's twinkling hazel eyes.

"I don't mind, Mattie. I would have been late, too, if I had a pair of roller skates." They both laughed, and with the laughter Caroline knew that her father had made the right choice in sending her to Saint Louis.

Mattie's boarding room was small, and its sleeping and adjoining sitting area were separated only by a movable rattan screen. At the end of the hall there was a necessary room with a tub for bathing, but it had to be shared with all the boarders on the second floor. For more immediate use, a white ironstone washbowl and water pitcher sat on top of an old washstand. And shoved under the bed was a chamber pot for late-night emergencies.

Though the flowers on the wallpaper had faded and the room had cheap furniture—a wrought-iron bed, a nightstand, a dented occasional table, a stained mirror, and a wooden box with a curtain that served as an armoire—Mattie had brightened it with some of her own belongings, including bright floral paintings on the walls, a rattan wing chair with a colorful chintz cushion, airy curtains, and a potted fern. The whole affair was hardly bigger than Caroline's bedroom at home, but she did not mind.

Already Caroline's spirits were high, and after an early dinner, Mattie changed into a split skirt and they strolled to the ice-cream parlor. With people bustling about on bicycles and occasionally buzzing by in loud, riotous automobiles, Caroline found herself laughing for the first time since her grandmother's death.

But that night, when loneliness caught up, Caroline could not sleep. She sat on top of one of her Saratoga trunks, which was big enough to serve as a window seat. Outside, moths flitted in erratic paths around the street lamps, and birds dived at them hungrily.

Mattie got up and sat beside her cousin.

"Do you miss your grandmother?" she asked softly.

Caroline nodded. "And Father. We were going to travel the world together, but..." Caroline let the words trail off and sighed.

Mattie hugged Caroline close, then held her at arm's length.

"Caroline Elizabeth Long, you've learned one of life's lessons very early, but that's all for the better."

"What lesson have I learned, Mattie?"

"Men can't be trusted. They'll say anything and promise anything."

Mattie's gaze drifted to a photograph on the nightstand. It was a handsome young man in a dashing Prince Albert coat.

"Was that your Philadelphy lawyer?" Caroline asked, nodding at the picture.

Mattie caught her breath, then picked up the ornate frame and looked at the young man with the walrus mustache. "Who called him a lawyer?" she asked.

"Ester."

Mattie laughed. "That sounds just like dear, sweet Ester. But Jonathan was not a lawyer, as he told me. He was just a clerk who filed papers and delivered messages. He hadn't two pennies to rub together."

"What happened to him?"

"Oh, I suppose he charged up San Juan Hill with Teddy Roosevelt. For all I know he got himself shot by a Spaniard. It would serve him right for being such a fool." She slammed the picture facedown on the stand, then turned to Caroline.

"I know you miss your father, but not to worry. Men really aren't necessary. A woman can get along nicely without one, if she plans a life of maidenhood. I shall never marry. I prefer to have a career."

"As a hello-girl?"

"Goodness, no." Mattie shook her head,

making her long, loose chestnut curls spill over her shoulders. "I want to become a novelist."

"Like the Brontë sisters?"

Mattie tilted her head and laughed. "No, silly goose. Those novels are for lovestruck girls with stars in their eyes. I want to write stories of intellect. Stories of human frailty and death."

Mattie's eyes glowed and her hands flew as she told Caroline the plot of one of her stories, in which everyone, including the heroine, the hero, the villain, and all the animals, died a horrid and confusing death that involved trains and railroad tracks.

Mattie's eyes glistened with tears as she described the final, tragic scene.

Caroline grimaced and swallowed hard. "They all died?"

"Yes, isn't it beautiful and profound?"

Caroline forced a smile. "I think I'm ready to go back to bed, Mattie. Thank you for the story."

As Caroline pulled the thin, worn quilt to her chin, she thought of the story Mattie had told her. She placed the silver heart-shaped frame with the picture of the Italian woman on the nightstand near the bed.

"Good night, Mother," she whispered. "Sleep with the angels."

That night Caroline dreamed of human frailty and death. And in her dream, a woman with long dark hair and dark eyes took her hand and smiled.

4

Mattie was dedicated to her constitution and walked every evening, come rain or shine, around six o'clock. Caroline had never met anyone with so much energy and ambition. Mattie's life was filled with one special event after another—lectures at the lyceum, visits to museums and libraries, political rallies, and women's suffrage marches. For entertainment she rode bicycles with Henry, roller-skated with Albert, attended the theater with Lawrence, and made trips to the ice-cream parlor with Philip. Caroline was sure that none of the young men knew that the others existed.

Mattie cared not one iota what others thought about her, and she wore split skirts where she pleased. She dared to play croquet on Sundays and even owned a bathing dress for public swimming.

But by the end of the first week, the excitement of the new surroundings began to wear off, and Caroline began to miss Taffy, Ester, Joshua, and the children. One day she borrowed some of Mattie's lilac-scented stationery. In clear, careful block print she wrote Taffy a long letter expounding on her trials and tribulations and begging Taffy to come to Saint Louis to visit. But when Caroline asked Mattie where the post office was, Mattie threw a fit and took the letter away.

"I'm sorry, Caroline," she said, "but if you mail that letter, Aunt Oriona will surely read it and know where you are. You don't want her coming here, do you? Heaven knows what she would do to me if she knew I was conspiring with your father to take care of you. Why, she might go so far as to have me arrested. You must keep your location a secret."

So though Caroline wrote letters to Taffy every few days, she did not mail them. She wrote letters to her father, too. He had hurt her, but still she could not break her old habit so easily. And she waited for his letters. But during Caroline's first month with her stepcousin, only one letter arrived from her father. It was addressed to Mattie and briefly stated that he was in New Orleans and all was going well.

The month of April arrived amidst a profusion of blooming flowers and swarming insects. Caroline was getting used to the daily routine. She attended public school now, rather than having a private tutor, and for the first time in her life she was surrounded by other children. Though the teacher liked Caroline and thought her intelligent, Caroline had not made any friends. The children asked rude questions about her parents and kinfolk. She couldn't answer their prying questions, and to avoid their stares, she took to eating her meals alone and sitting in the back row, against the wall.

One day after school, during a heated game of marbles in which Caroline won a prized agate from Mrs. Carraway's oldest boy, Conor, the irate redhead called her a mulatto. Caroline threw a rock at him and it smacked his freckled nose, drawing blood. Another time, an annoying schoolgirl with bouncy blond hair called Caroline a darkie. Again the rocks flew and the blood dripped. After that, the teacher no longer gave Caroline preferential treatment and threatened to have her expelled.

Caroline grew to despise school and looked for any excuse to miss it. By the first week in May, her studies had grown boring and she'd begun counting the days until school would be dismissed for the summer.

One balmy Saturday afternoon Caroline walked beside Mattie, who was dressed in a new Turkish skirt with loose, puffy folds that billowed over her knees. The day was lovely, with flowers blooming and birds singing and a delicious fresh spring breeze. Women and gentlemen promenaded up and down the boulevards to show off their latest finery. The street bustled with carriages, buggies, wagons, and an occasional motorcar filled with laughing people wearing eye goggles, smocks called dusters, and veils or neck scarves.

As Caroline and Mattie rounded a corner, they heard a *tap-tap-tap* and saw two teenage boys. One youth held a large stack of colorful posters; the other had shimmied up a wooden pole and was nailing a poster onto it. After finishing, he dusted off his knickerbockers and moved down the street to the next pole. Up and down the avenue, boys were shoving small handbills into the fists of every pedestrian they saw. Caroline noticed that one of the boys was Mrs. Carraway's son Conor.

Farther down the block, a man was pasting up a tremendously large colored poster on the side of an abandoned building. A crowd had gathered around him.

"What is that poster advertising?" Caroline asked, wondering what could make the crowd buzz with excitement so quickly.

"Let's get closer and see," Mattie said. They pushed through the crowd just as the man was smoothing down the last section with his long-handled brush.

"It's announcing Shawnee Sam's Wild West Extravaganza," Caroline said, after reading the words. "How exciting, Mattie. Have you ever attended a Wild West show?"

"Yes, I saw Shawnee Sam's show right here in Saint Louis. Goodness, it was over fourteen years ago, when I was a girl about your age. Your grandmother, your aunt Oriona, your father, and I made a weekend excursion of it.

We rode a train all the way to Saint Louis. This was before you were born, of course. Wild West shows were very new back then. They stop at the big towns, and many of them come through Saint Louis. Of course, the most famous and grandest of all is Buffalo Bill's Wild West program, but I've never seen that one.

"We were extremely curious about Shawnee Sam's show, especially your father. He actually became so fascinated that he ran away while we were here and took a job as a roustabout for the month the show was in Saint Louis. Oriona thought it scandalous. Your grandmother wasn't pleased, but she thought it might do her son good to hold down a job for a while. He was quite the reckless gallant back then."

"Did you enjoy the show? Was it exciting?" Caroline bristled with anticipation. She had heard that her father had worked in a Wild West show, but her grandmother and aunt and father had refused to tell her any details.

"Actually, I didn't care for it. I was a very timid child back then and almost broke out in hives from the smoke and noise of the awful, loud guns of those sharpshooters. And those smelly cows and buffalo snorting about. I guess I shall always be a city girl," Mattie said with a laugh.

While they were talking, Conor Carraway ran up to Caroline and shoved a small handbill at her. It was not colorful like the posters, but printed with black ink on cheap, bright yellow paper.

"Here you go, Miss Dusty Face."

"What are you doing?" Caroline asked.

"I'm earnin' meself a free ticket to the Wild West show, that's what," the boy bragged, and hustled up to the next unsuspecting person.

Caroline studied the wall poster with its colorful cowboys, horses, buffalo, and Indians wearing long headdresses.

"What do you think of Shawnee Sam's show?" Mattie asked her.

"I'm not sure. In a way, it looks frightening."

"Frankly, I'm surprised you aren't begging to see it, considering."

Caroline turned to her cousin, her eyebrows all crinkled up. "Considering what?"

"Considering your mother."

Caroline felt the blood drain from her face. Mattie cocked her head to one side and crossed her arms.

"Surely Jackson or your grandmother told you that your mother performed in Shawnee Sam's Wild West show. Your father met her that summer."

"They told me she was in a Wild West show. But no one told me it was Shawnee Sam's show. They won't even tell me my mother's name or anything else about her. All I know is that she was a beautiful Italian lady, with noble blood. And she rode a dancing horse."

"They told you she was Italian nobility?"

Caroline nodded slowly.

Mattie's face churned like a storm-tossed sea, then she took her cousin's hand.

"Child, I don't know all the lies your grandmother and Oriona have told you, but if you want to know the truth about your mother, there is something you need to see."

Caroline's heart raced as she followed her cousin back to the boardinghouse and up the narrow stairs. Mattie opened the old trunk that Onita had given Caroline. As she opened it, the smells of dust and old clothes and books and mementos of years past filled the air.

"I was rummaging through this one day while you were playing marbles with Mrs. Carraway's children," Mattie said. "I hope you don't mind."

"No, to tell you the truth, I've not looked at the contents yet. Taffy said it's just a bunch of old souvenirs. It reminds me too much of Grandmother and makes me sad."

At last Mattie reached the bottom of the trunk and removed a rolled-up cylinder of thick paper. She unfurled it gently, then placed a book on each corner so that it lay flat on top of her bed. It was a small poster, not from a circus, as Caroline had thought the first time she saw it in Taffy's hands, but from Shawnee Sam's Wild West Extravaganza.

Mattie lit the kerosene lamp and held it close to the colorful poster.

"This is your mother," she said, pointing to a woman on a white horse.

Caroline felt her knees go weak and she crumpled into a chair.

5

The woman in the poster was beautiful. Her eyes were blacker than night and stared intently ahead at some unseen object. Her long snake-like braids of black hair flew out from her head as she balanced her small, trim body on the back of a white horse. Her buckskin costume and moccasins glittered with elaborate bead patterns, and a small feather headdress rested on her finely shaped head. Around her neck hung the same beaded neckband that Caroline had found so interesting. In the background, a dozen or more Indian warriors wearing feather bonnets watched her in stoic silence. The caption beneath the painting read PRINCESS DANC-ING RAIN.

"But this can't be my mother. This woman is an Indian," Caroline said in disbelief.

"I am so sorry," Mattie said. "They should have told you."

"I didn't know she was an Indian." Caroline whispered, for her mouth had gone dry.

"But how did Aunt Onita explain your dark features? Surely you knew that you had mixed blood. Not that it makes a difference to me. But after all, it is...well, my dear cousin, it is obvious." Mattie lowered her voice to a whisper and glanced at the door. "All those times they chastised you for getting in the sun, all those times they made you wear gloves and a bonnet and carry a parasol...I remember once you were playing with Taffy and a nosy old biddy made some comment to Aunt Onita about you being Taffy's half sister. After that, she never let you out unsupervised. How did she explain it to you?"

"Italian." Caroline barely managed to get the word out. "They told me Mother was Italian royalty. Sometimes Aunt Oriona said my mother was a gypsy, but Father denied it. This must be a mistake. What makes you think this Indian woman is my mother? Father would have told me. Father…" A sinking feeling gripped Caroline's heart. She sighed heavily, then tore her eyes from the poster and looked into Mattie's worried face. "Did you know my mother?"

Mattie squeezed her young cousin's hands. "Let's have some tea first, and then I'll tell you all I know."

They walked downstairs to the kitchen, and Mattie boiled water and prepared the tea. She carried it back upstairs and served it alongside some of Mrs. Carraway's shortbread.

"Of course, I saw your mother perform in the Wild West show," Mattie said, after settling onto the settee and sipping the hot liquid. "She was extraordinarily graceful and acrobatic. She stood up on that white horse as if the feat were no more difficult than walking. Then she crawled under the horse's stomach or turned around or leaped off and on doing all kinds of tricks—oh, I can't recall everything she did." Mattie sipped her tea slowly. "After the show, I only saw your mother once, briefly. She came to the house one night in a terrible rainstorm. She was exhausted and on the verge of childbirth. Aunt Onita sent Joshua to fetch Dr.

Lewis, but he was away on an emergency—the rain had washed away the footbridge and several people had fallen into the raging river. So Joshua ran to the colored part of town to fetch the midwife who had delivered his own daughter a couple of weeks before."

"That baby was Taffy. She's only two weeks older than I am."

"Unfortunately, by the time the midwife arrived, your mother had already been laboring for almost two hours. She had ridden a horse all the way from Illinois, through terrible rainstorms, to reach your grandmother's house."

"And Father was with her. They got married in another town, but he brought Mother home just for my birth, so we could live with Grandmother in a proper house. Father said..."

Caroline stopped speaking when she saw the expression on her cousin's face and the shaking head.

"What's wrong, Mattie?" she asked in a tiny voice.

"There, there." Mattie patted Caroline's hand. "I know all this is much for a young girl, but you might as well know the whole truth all at once, rather than have it dribbled out to you piecemeal. Have another cup of tea, and take courage."

Caroline sipped the steaming tea and felt its warmth flow down her throat, but it could not chase away the icy fear building in her heart.

"Do you want me to continue?" Mattie asked softly.

Caroline nodded and braced herself for the truth.

"Part of your father's story is true. Jackson did fall in love with your mother while he worked in the Wild West show. But unfortunately, he did not marry her. To the poor boy's credit, I'm sure he did not know about her condition when the show left Saint Louis and traveled east. Had he known, surely he would have married her. But nonetheless, when her condition became obvious it must have caused great shame for her family, for she was apparently forced to leave the show. She was very clever and tracked your father down. She was a renegade, you know. Indians were not allowed off their reservations without permission back then. She lived off the land as she traveled all the way from Illinois to Missouri. But the trip was hard on her, especially those last few days. The rains that spring were the worst we'd seen in ages. She was half-dead with pneumonia when she collapsed on your grandmother's front porch. There was nothing the midwife could do except ensure that the baby was born."

Caroline heard a clicking noise and looked down at the teacup rattling in her trembling hands. She put it down.

"There, there. Be brave." Mattie pulled Caroline close and patted her shoulder.

"So I was an unwanted child. Grandmother lied to me all these years. And Father..." Rage swelled up inside Caroline, and she rose to her feet. "Is there more, Mattie? What other secrets did they keep from me?"

"Are you sure you want to know?"

Caroline swallowed hard, then crumpled back into the chair.

"Yes, I must know everything."

"Your grandmother accepted you and loved you. You were sickly at first but developed into a sweet, darling baby, and she grew to love you like her own. You brought joy and happiness into your grandmother's life—never doubt that for a moment."

Caroline sighed with relief and imagined her grandmother's sweet, round face all crinkled with smiles as she waved her hands and swayed her head and tapped her foot in rhythm to her students' music lessons.

"Thank you, Mattie. That bit of truth was the honey; now what bitter medicine do you have to accompany it?"

"Well, to put it kindly, let us just say that your father was very young—only nineteen—and far too spoiled and restless to settle down and take care of an infant. He had hardly come out of childhood himself, and the responsibility was too much. He took off on the first of his wild money-making adventures. It broke your grandmother's heart, but as usual, she forgave him when he returned two years later, penniless and begging for money. She had hoped that seeing how lovely you were would make him take his fatherly duties seriously, but I'm afraid that a lifetime of being a spoiled child could not be undone so swiftly.

"And that is how things continued. Jackson would return every year or so to get more funding for some new wild scheme. I know your father loves you, Caroline, in his own way, but he is truly an irresponsible man. But then, I suppose all men are irresponsible." She sighed and sipped her tea, her eyes focused on the tiny photo of the dashing young man in the Prince Albert coat.

"How long have you known about my mother?"

"Since you were born."

"And I suppose even Ester and Joshua knew?"

"Yes, of course. Ester helped with the birthing, and Joshua carried your mother's body to the cemetery for a quick burial. It's an unmarked grave, I'm sorry to say."

"Then everyone knew except me!" The pain of the truth raged through Caroline like a prairie whirlwind. She wanted to scream, to throw things across the room. "Why didn't someone tell me? And all this time Aunt Oriona kept calling my mother a gypsy. How often I longed to go without a hat and parasol, running in the sunshine like an ordinary girl. Now I see why they made me stay in the shade. They were afraid that my skin would turn as brown as a berry. They were ashamed of me."

"Caroline, your mother was an Indian,

true, but that changes nothing in my eyes. Nor in the eyes of your grandmother. She loved you for yourself, because you are a sweet, generous child with a loving heart. Try not to be bitter."

Caroline stared at the poster a moment longer, then quickly rolled it back up into a tight cylinder and tied it with a red hair ribbon. In a frenzy of passion, she rummaged through the trunk where she kept her valuables, pulling out every picture, every memento of Italy that she had collected. The miniature gondolas from Venice, the small marble statue from Rome, the lava rocks from Pompeii... She opened the heart-shaped silver frame and ripped out the picture of the dark-haired Italian opera singer. All these things were meaningless now.

While Mattie took an afternoon nap, Caroline stuffed all the Italian souvenirs in a knapsack and took them to a curio shop. The owner paid her three dollars for the lot. She also took the beaded neckband that had belonged to her mother. It looked obviously savage in design now. How could she have ever thought it was an Italian pattern? The shop owner eyed the necklace and made a decent offer, but Caroline changed her mind and withdrew it. After all, she reasoned, she could not blame her mother for anything. Had she lived, perhaps Caroline's life would have been very different. Maybe she would have been raised by her mother's people and at this very moment would be sitting in a tepee eating buffalo meat or corn.

For hours Caroline wandered through the streets of Saint Louis scandalously unaccompanied, drawing stares of disapproval and many questions from strangers concerned that she was lost. Men and women pedaled by on bicycles, ringing the tiny bells on the handlebars, and even a noisy Duryea motorcar passed by her unnoticed.

Just as the lamplighter was turning up the gas lights along a boulevard that had not yet gone to electric lampposts, Caroline found herself in front of the wall-sized poster advertising the upcoming Shawnee Sam Wild West Extravaganza. She stared at the cowboys and buffalo, and at the Indians racing across the scene. Some warriors wore feather bonnets reaching the ground; others were younger men with war paint streaked across their bare arms and legs. Nowhere in the poster did she see an Indian woman on a white horse—or any Indian women at all, for that matter.

Caroline thought about the poster from Grandmother Long's trunk. Perhaps her mother had been a rare exception, a woman more talented than anyone else in the show. She surely had been the most beautiful. The poster was only a lithograph of a painting, and as such was probably not entirely accurate, but still Dancing Rain was a woman whom people would remember.

As Caroline walked back to the boardinghouse, a plan began to creep into her head. She walked slowly at first, dragging her feet, but as the plan took shape, her footsteps grew faster and bolder. When she at last arrived at the boardinghouse, she ran up the wooden porch steps.

"Here she is!" shouted one of the redheaded boys. "She's come back!"

"Caroline! Where have you been?" Mattie's voice quavered as she threw her arms around her cousin. "I've called the police. They've been searching for you." Mattie dragged her cousin into the drawing room. "Now, young lady, explain yourself!"

"I have a plan," Caroline said slowly. "I'm

going to attend the Wild West show next week and find someone who knew my mother. I'm going to find out everything I can about her and find her family."

"Her family no doubt lives in a tepee on a reservation in the middle of the prairie."

"That doesn't matter. I must find out about her anyway."

Mattie twirled a strand of chestnut hair around her finger impatiently.

"I've heard that the show now enacts an Indian massacre of helpless pioneers and other horrendous deeds. Are you certain you want to see such scenes of degradation?"

"But all that isn't real, Mattie. No one truly gets killed. It's no different than going to the theater to watch a Shakespeare play and seeing Macbeth covered with blood after killing the king."

Mattie put her hands on her hips.

"You do make a point, Caroline. But Shake-spearean violence occurs offstage, out of the sight of tender young eyes. A pioneer massacre in broad daylight is something entirely different. It might cause you great stress."

"You watched a Wild West show when you

were my age." Caroline crossed her arms and stuck her chin in the air.

Mattie hesitated, speechless for a moment.

"I will pay for the ticket with my own money," Caroline continued. "I sold my Italian souvenirs and have enough for a ticket, a program, and perhaps even some mementos. I may never get this chance again in my entire life. Please, Mattie. Give me your blessing and don't try to stop me."

"You are persistent, Miss Caroline Long," Mattie said at last. "Very well, you may go if Mrs. Carraway agrees to chaperone you. I am working during the week and cannot do so. And on Saturday, Mr. James Rothington the Third has invited me to accompany him in a game of golf."

Mrs. Carraway, pausing at the door with an armful of fresh linens, drew in a sharp breath, then giggled.

"Now, there's a fine catch for any young lady. Has his own motorcar, he has."

Caroline turned to the plump redheaded woman in the lacy white apron.

"Will you take me, Mrs. Carraway? I won't be any trouble."

"Of course you won't be, me little darlin'. Me boy Conor has tickets for the last performance. You're welcome to sit by me side."

Caroline gave Mrs. Carraway a big squeeze. She heard Mattie sigh.

"All right, then, you can go. But I do not know what you hope to gain by this. It has been fourteen years since your mother traveled with Shawnee Sam's show. It was not the best of the Wild West shows, far inferior to Buffalo Bill's. It's almost a miracle that he's still in business and still coming to Saint Louis."

"It's more than a miracle, Mattie. It's fate."

"I'm not so sure of that. The odds of someone remembering your mother are so remote it borders on the impossible. Are you sure you want to waste your money on this enterprise?"

"Yes, with all my heart. It is a chance I must take or I'll regret it the rest of my life. I must know about my mother."

"It is my personal feeling that the less you know about your mother and her people, the better off you will be. But I understand that longing in your heart. My own mother died when I was very young. I regret not knowing her side of the family." Mattie paused. "You must promise me that you will not be too disappointed if you do not find any information about your mother, and that you will let the matter rest afterward."

"I promise." Caroline threw her arms around Mattie's waist. "If no one remembers her, then I will not pursue the matter."

The rest of the week, Caroline listened to every conversation she could about the Wild West Extravaganza. She read every newspaper article printed and collected every handbill or fancy printed courier she could find. Shawnee Sam's show, when compared to the larger and more famous ones, like those of Buffalo Bill Cody or Pawnee Bill, was found to be lacking. There were not as many crack shots or skilled ropers or cowboys or Indians. And none of the Indians were famous warriors like Sitting Bull, or Red Cloud, or Spotted Tail, who had all traveled with Wild West shows at one time or another. But Caroline did not care.

Every day that passed brought with it a nervous anticipation that defied description. It was not the gleeful sensation a child feels while waiting for an occasion such as Christmas, which is sure to bring gifts. Rather, Caroline's feelings were more akin to those of a bride anticipating her wedding day with an unknown groom.

The night before the show arrived in town, Caroline tossed and turned. She paced the hallways in her nightdress and peeked out the door and up the street for some sign of the colorful red-and-gold wagons. She unfurled the old poster dozens of times, scrutinizing her mother's face.

In the early morning hours on the day of the show's arrival, Caroline lit a candle and stared at her own face in the mirror. Her eyes were not as black as her mother's and her dark hair had bouncy curls. Her lips weren't as full, nor was her face quite as broad. If she had aunts and uncles and cousins and grandparents living somewhere, would they even recognize her? But more than that, would they accept her as one of their own?

6

The May sunshine bathed the downtown buildings in gold and warmed the spring flowers planted in boxes around street lamps. In the noisy crowd lining both sides of the street, small children bounced up and down in their parents' arms. Annoying boys wove between legs or climbed onto every available tree, roof, or pole along the parade route. Policemen blew whistles and pushed people back as the anticipation became almost unbearable.

Caroline wore her favorite blouse, of pink-and-white stripes with a broad sailor's collar, tucked into a wine-colored skirt, with white stockings and jersey button-up gaiters over her shoes. On her head perched a straw hat festooned with fresh daisies. Mattie, defying the stares of the older women, bravely wore baggy Turkish trousers with a neat short jacket and tie. Though Mattie insisted she did not want to see the Wild West show, she had agreed to watch the grand entry parade.

Caroline and Mrs. Carraway's oldest son had arrived early to secure a wonderful location for viewing. Caroline put down two stools, one for Mattie and one for Mrs. Carraway, but she herself could not sit still. Besides, a woman with a hat smothered in feathers, flowers, and a bird's nest blocked her view when Caroline was sitting down.

"Here it comes!" Mrs. Carraway's son shouted, and the crowd exploded with applause.

First came the band, men dressed in black-and-gray uniforms, wearing cowboy hats and riding high atop a bandwagon pulled by perfectly matched, lovely white horses. They switched from ragtime tunes like "There'll Be a Hot Time in the Old Town Tonight" to old-time sentimental favorites by Stephen Foster to the bouncy "Buffalo Gals."

After the band, three trains of mules

clomped down the street pulling specially made gold-colored wagons emblazoned with red letters on the side that proclaimed SHAWNEE SAM'S WILD WEST EXTRAVAGANZA.

Rows of mounted roughriders and cowboys rode behind the wagons, waving to the cheering crowd. Next came several Mexican vaqueros twirling lariats. The mayor's wife and two prominent citizens waved from the window of a stagecoach drawn by beautifully matched black horses. From the back of a Conestoga wagon, a family dressed in plain homespun pioneer clothing waved merrily.

Directly behind the wagons, a grubby band of mountain men in buckskins and raccoon-skin hats talked and spit tobacco juice as they walked by, every now and then making a face at a child in the crowd or pointing a muzzle-loading rifle at an imaginary bear in a tree.

Next, looking very dignified in their long black coats, pants, and hats, three sharpshooters rode by in silence. In the lead, sitting straight and proud on top of a glorious Appaloosa stallion, Shawnee Sam waved to the crowd, his long blond hair flowing in the wind like that of a character from a dime novel. A stout woman sharpshooter, wearing a short jacket and split gaucho pants that hugged her plump figure, occasionally shot a pistol. At the sound of the loud pops, women in the crowd screamed, little babies cried, and the boys in the trees whooped in glee.

Caroline waved and shouted merrily as each new group paraded down the street. She enjoyed everything she saw, but it was not until the end of the parade that Caroline's heart began to pound so fast that she could hardly breathe.

At last the Indians were coming by, some on foot, some on horses of every spotted pattern imaginable and decorated with paint. The older men wore brilliant feather headdresses that cascaded down their backs. Fringes of rawhide and clumps of long black hair dangled from their buckskin shirts and pants and lances. Their beaded moccasins and belts and neck pendants twinkled in the morning sun. Some of the younger braves wore no shirts, allowing their bronze skin to display painted figures and secret symbols. Lastly came the Indian women, on foot, some carrying papooses on their backs. They did not wave, nor did they seem to care about the crowd gawking and pointing at them.

Caroline scrutinized the men and women, and in each and every face saw her own eyes and nose and cheekbones. She wanted to run to them and shout at the top of her voice, "I am the daughter of Princess Dancing Rain. Does anyone here remember her?"

But in truth, the sight of the feathers, the muscular brown arms carrying bows and arrows and tomahawks, the painted faces, stern and unsmiling, and the smell of the deerskins and feather bonnets all gave Caroline chill bumps and made her feel dizzy. Not one of the grim faces smiled at the crowd, but they stared ahead solemnly. Only one of the Indians looked in her direction, an older man with gray hair that tumbled to his waist. His black eyes bored into hers for a few seconds, then he turned away.

Mattie, who had gotten up from her stool, fanned herself furiously.

"Oh, dear. I am beginning to remember the smells and sounds of the Wild West show again." She grimaced. "It seems like a lifetime ago, not fourteen years, that I sat in the front row of the arena, smelling the reek of horse manure and axle grease and buckskin clothing. And those awful gunshots ringing in my ears..." She turned up her nose as a horse suddenly sidestepped and rudely swished its tail into the crowd. "I think the parade is enough to satisfy my taste for the Wild West show. I definitely shall not attend."

But Caroline hungered for more sights and sounds and smells, even unpleasant ones. She wanted to follow the parade to the fairgrounds, but Mattie refused to let her, for it was Saturday and she had planned for them both to attend an art lecture at the lyceum. Reluctantly Caroline walked home, listening to Mrs. Carraway's children carry on about the parade.

"Did you see the Injuns?" the middle boy said to his mother. "Betcha those were real scalps tied to their belts. We'd better lock the doors and windows tonight, Ma."

The youngest girl burst into tears and clung to her mother's skirt.

"I'm afeered of Injuns," she wailed.

Caroline wanted to toss the child into the river but refrained from opening her mouth. She would have to be on her best behavior for two whole weeks, for the last Saturday of the show was the only day that Mrs. Carraway could get away to attend as Caroline's chaperone.

They were the longest two weeks in Caroline's life, she was sure. Each day dragged and tormented her with daily newspaper stories recounting the exciting events of the show. Shawnee Sam's Wild West Extravaganza seemed to be on the lips of every couple at the ice-cream parlor, every gentleman riding a bicycle in the evening, every child playing hoops in the street. Caroline despised having to wait until the last day, and she constantly worried that the show might leave early, without warning, or that something might happen to Mrs. Carraway.

But at long last the day arrived, and Caroline sat under a massive canvas tent on a stiff wooden bleacher near the far end of the hippodrome. Her heart pounded as the grand review entered the arena—dozens of colorful cowboys, and roughriders, and Indians on running horses, carrying American flags and banners of extraordinary beauty. The older Indians wore elaborate warbonnets that flowed behind them in the wind as they whooped and waved tomahawks. Caroline shivered and hugged herself.

When the show began, Caroline did not know what she was looking for but had an intuition that she would recognize whatever it was. Many women in the audience turned their heads at the sight of the bloodcurdling pioneer massacre reenactment, but Mrs. Carraway, a hefty woman with a strong heart, was not intimidated by scenes of death. She had been orphaned in Ireland after losing most of her family during the potato famine.

Caroline enjoyed the stagecoach attack, the talented sharpshooters, the bronco riders and bull ropers, but it was the Indian dancing that fascinated her the most. The crowd shuddered when a teenage Indian boy danced with a live snake; it applauded when several Comanche boys raced their spotted ponies around the hippodrome.

One very old man performed a mock rain dance. From behind the bleachers someone rattled a tin sheet to imitate thunder. Shawnee Sam rode up and stopped the old man from bringing rain, saying that he didn't want the good folks in the audience to get wet walking to their homes. The old man, listed on the program as "Billy Big Tree, The Wichita Shaman," did not appear to be very happy about being stopped. He glared at Shawnee Sam, made some signs in the air, then left the arena with great indignation.

The show's grand finale brought back to life Custer's Last Charge at Little Bighorn, a blatant copy of Buffalo Bill Cody's Wild West and Congress of Rough Riders of the World show. But while Cody's show used mostly Sioux, some of whom actually took part in the real battle, Caroline had read in the newspapers that Shawnee Sam's show used Indians from mostly southern tribes living in Indian Territory. And besides that, Buffalo Bill Cody's grand finale was now an enactment of the charge up San Juan Hill led by Teddy Roosevelt. Everything about Shawnee Sam's show was a copy of something from Buffalo Bill's or Pawnee Bill's famous shows. The newspaper reviewer called Sam's show a "second-rate imitation with less talented performers, less interesting acts, and the most pitiful-looking

Indians." But Caroline did not agree. Every horse, every cowboy, every Indian looked grand and noble to her.

After the show, while Mrs. Carraway became engaged in a lively conversation with one of her boarders, Caroline easily slipped away unnoticed. Ladies in fine walking dresses and gentlemen in suits and hats strolled around the pitched tents and temporary corrals while boys in knickerbockers darted uncontrolled about the grounds. The smells of cow and buffalo manure and fresh hay permeated the air, as well as the pungent odor of tobacco juice, which covered the ground where men had recently spit. Hardly could a woman step without seeing a wad of tobacco or a puddle of the dark offensive juice.

While Caroline was petting an overly friendly mule that was fascinated with her straw hat, she spied the teenage Indian boy who had performed in the snake dance. She remembered him because he was tall and wore a small cluster of bright red and black feathers fastened to the back of his head. His hair was cropped very short on the right side of his head but flowed past his shoulders on the left side.

The moment that the curious mule grabbed Caroline's straw hat in its massive jaws, she screamed. The boy spun around, his earrings and metal trinkets jingling.

"Oh, you naughty beast," Caroline said angrily, and fought the mule for what was left of her hat. But her slender fingers were no match for the mule's heavy jaws and huge yellow teeth.

The people around her snickered, but not one of them came to her rescue, except for the young Indian with the painted face. He did something to the mule's mouth and the hat dropped to the ground. He swooped down to pick it up, brushed it off, and offered it to Caroline.

"Your hat, miss," he said in perfect English with just a touch of an accent.

Caroline stared at the pathetic piece of lopsided straw, sighed heavily, then shoved it back at the mule.

"You might as well have it all," she said to the animal, then angrily pushed back a few loose curls from her face. "Doesn't Shawnee Sam feed his livestock?" she asked.

The boy's dark eyes stared in mild curiosity

from behind a face painted with yellow, red, and white stripes. Designs in the same colors decorated his bronze chest and arms.

"Yes, but a mule has a mind of its own. This one has good taste in hats, I think." His speech was slow, even, and deliberate. Caroline couldn't be sure if he was joking, except for his twinkling dark eyes. She felt her face get hot and wished she had brought Mattie's little fan.

"Well, thank you for trying to salvage it. I've just about outgrown the hat, anyway. Now I'll have a good excuse to buy another."

Caroline smiled, then could not think of another word to say. After sitting for hours and waiting for days for the opportunity to speak to an Indian, she found herself speechless. The boy didn't speak, either. As he shifted his weight and turned to leave, Caroline drew in a breath.

"Was that a live snake?" she blurted out.

His eyes clouded, as if he had received a great insult.

"Of course it was alive," Caroline quickly answered her own question. "I meant to say, was that snake poisonous?"

"What would a man prove by dancing with a toothless snake?"

"I see your point. Then it was...uh... what kind of snake?"

He spoke some words in his language, then said, "Rattlesnake."

"You are very brave. What makes you want to dance with a snake? Is it a special ceremony of your people?"

The boy chuckled, then glanced over his shoulder. "No," he whispered, "but don't tell anyone. It was Shawnee Sam's idea. I think he made it up just to scare the ladies in the audience. Do you like snakes?"

Caroline had seen only little green garden snakes in her life and thought them sweet and playful.

"Yes, I adore snakes," she said quickly, happy to be carrying on a conversation.

"Then you will want to see the rattlesnake. I keep it in this box." He held up a wooden box with airholes in its top and sides.

Caroline swallowed hard. She had heard of rattlesnakes and had seen drawings of them in Aunt Oriona's nature books, but she had no desire to meet one face-to-face. Yet she did not want to look like a silly goose afraid of her own shadow.

"Yes, let me see it." She tried to hide her nervousness with a weak smile.

He slowly opened the box. The snake hissed and its rattle shook. Caroline froze for a moment, not breathing nor blinking as her heart thumped in her chest. She wanted to scream and run, but something told her that this was a test of courage and she refused to be intimidated. After a few seconds, the boy slammed the lid shut and clasped the latch. His eyes studied her closely, but he did not speak.

"Snakes are beautiful in their own way," Caroline said at last, feeling a drop of perspiration slide down her temple, "but I must admit, I prefer the bison. They are magnificent creatures."

The boy nodded and looked in the direction of the menagerie, where many species of animals were penned—buffalo, deer, antelope, Texas longhorns, sheep and goats, and a bear on a chain.

"Buffalo are the most magnificent animals ever created. Want to see one up close?"

"Oh yes, yes! I would love to touch the

woolly heads and look into the black eyes. They seem so tiny and beady. Are bison cruel animals?" Caroline's tongue found its second wind and rattled on as she followed the boy, being careful to avoid the box with the airholes that he swung by his side. Metal trinkets and beads jingled with each step he took.

Two Indian men wearing soft deerskin clothing stood by a temporary corral that contained three bison. The men were taking money from parents, then lifting children over the rails so that they could touch the dark, hairy hides. Caroline's heart sank. Was this just a ruse that all the Indians used to get a few extra pennies and nickels? She knew that she had not a single copper penny on her person. The embarrassment would be unbearable if the boy asked for money. She stopped.

"Oh, dear, it looks so crowded. Perhaps I should come back later."

"No bother. Those two men tending the buffalo are my uncles. I can come and go as I please." He tilted his head toward the pen. "I promise the buffalo won't harm you. They're old and weak."

Caroline did not know what to say, but she

knew that it would be rude not to accept his invitation. He pressed through the crowd and, after setting his snake box on the ground and removing his noisy foot bands, he crawled through the wooden rails. He spoke to one of his uncles in their language. The man did not seem pleased to see his nephew and glared at Caroline with hawkish eyes.

"Give me your hand," the boy said on returning to Caroline's side.

Caroline extended her hand, gloved in white to match her stockings, and crawled through the fence rails. Several women whispered and frowned. Some children pointed at her rudely, but soon their stares were forgotten as Caroline stood beside a monstrously large female bison.

"This is a very old, gentle cow," the boy said. "She has been with the show for years. Sometimes my uncle rides on her back for fun. But I do not recommend it."

Caroline quickly removed her glove. The moment her hand touched the bison's face something passed through her body.

"She is sad," Caroline said. "She misses running free on the prairie with her family. She misses the taste of sweet spring grass and the coolness of stream water on her lips. She is very old and tired. She wants to go back to the prairie to die. Poor beast." Caroline stroked the woolly head and the wet black nose.

The Indian boy stared at Caroline a moment, then took her elbow and led her back to the other side of the corral.

"Have you always talked with animals?" he asked slowly.

Caroline shrugged. "I have a horse—I mean, I *had* a horse—and sometimes it was as if I could read his mind. And Mrs. Carraway's cat is easy to predict. I don't know that I'm communicating; I just know that I love animals and it isn't hard to imagine what they feel. Of course, I don't think they are really talking to me—do you?"

"Yes, I do. One who talks with the animals has great power and can become a shaman. I've never heard of a white person who had this power."

His black eyes stared at Caroline relentlessly, and she thought perhaps he was going to ask her if she was part Indian. Though she was used to being called an olive-complexioned person at home, next to him her skin looked pale.

"Thank you for showing me the bison," Caroline said.

The boy grunted and paused. Caroline sensed that he was waiting for payment. Her head churned in a panic, then suddenly she remembered a pearl button that had come off her sleeve earlier that day. She had slipped it into her handbag. Mattie would absolutely, positively go into a conniption if she knew that Caroline was thinking of giving away a pearl button, but she had no other choice. She removed it from her bag and held it out to the young Indian.

"What is that?" he asked.

"It's your payment. I don't have any money, but the button is quite expensive."

The boy's face blushed under the striped paint.

"I did not ask you for money."

"But the other Indians were taking money for allowing children to pet the buffalo. I thought it was the custom..."

"You thought I was being kind and civil to you only in hopes of getting money? That is typical of White Man's thinking. Why don't you just offer me a cheap glass bead and laugh in my face?" He spun on his heel.

Caroline's lips parted in shock. How could she have misjudged him so cruelly?

"Please wait! I'm sorry. I didn't mean to insult you." Caroline trotted after him, and the women's whispers filled the air.

A stout gentleman in a top hat blocked her path. "Young lady, you are disgracing yourself chasing after that savage." He took Caroline's arm and led her away from the corrals. "Where is your mother?"

"She is over there," Caroline lied. She broke free and walked toward a strange matronly woman. She said hello to the plump woman, then kept on walking around the tents and back lots until she had circled the fairgrounds and arrived back at the buffalo corral. The crowd had thinned considerably and the animals were eagerly feasting on bundles of golden hay.

Caroline waited until the last spectator had left. She patted the old buffalo cow and sighed so loudly that the animal pricked her ears and stepped back in fright. Caroline turned over an old wooden bucket and sat on it, her chin resting in her hands.

She imagined that Mrs. Carraway was hysterical by now and had probably gone home to tell Mattie that her cousin had vanished. They might even call the police and form a search party, and no doubt they thought the most horrendous things had happened, but Caroline could not move from the bucket. Maybe it was going to be harder than she thought to find information about her mother. Maybe she was wasting her time being here at all.

But at last her patience was rewarded by the soft tread of moccasins and the jingle of silver bells behind her.

"Why are you still here?" The familiar Indian boy walked in front of Caroline and folded his arms.

"I stayed because I had to tell you I'm sorry," she said, standing up. "Please accept my apology."

He didn't move or speak.

"I'll stay here all night unless you forgive me," she said, and crossed her arms, too. He fought back a smile and made a sign with his right hand.

"Does that mean you forgive me?" Caroline asked.

"No, it means you are crazy." He pulled up another bucket and overturned it next to hers. "What do they call you?"

"Caroline. And you?"

"Crooked Feather."

"That's a strange name. Why would your parents name you that?"

"They didn't name me that when I was born. I earned the name when I had lived but eight winters. On the reservation where I was born there is a small lake, with a tall cottonwood tree growing on its banks, and in the uppermost branches is an eagles' nest. One day I saw that three eaglets had hatched. An eaglet is a thing of great value. It can be captured and raised."

"Why would you want to capture an eagle? Do you eat them?"

"Of course not. We value them greatly for their beauty, strength, and feathers. So one day I decided to climb the cottonwood tree and steal one of the baby eagles."

"Did you want to raise a pet, like a dog?"

Crooked Feather clamped his mouth shut and glared at Caroline.

"Has anyone ever told you that it is rude to interrupt a man telling a story?"

"Sorry. I didn't know." Caroline looked at her toes a moment and waited for him to continue his story.

"As I climbed the tree, the mother eagle swooped down and attacked me. I swatted at her and grabbed one of her tail feathers. By the time I reached the ground, I was cut and scratched from her talons. And the feather in my hand was all smashed and crooked, but I wore it proudly in my hair anyway." He pointed to a dark brown feather tipped in white that was the focal point in his small crown of red and black feathers. "That is why they call me Crooked Feather. Why do they call you Caroline? What is the story behind your name? I will listen quietly while you tell me."

Caroline rubbed her chin a moment. "No one has ever told me why I am named Caroline. I guess I was named after one of the Carolina states."

"You were named after a state?"

"I think my grandparents were born there.

I don't really like my name, but there's nothing I can do about it."

"Names are very important. They tell people who you are and what you've done. Why don't you choose another name?"

"I can't name myself!"

"Of course you can. Has any event happened in your life that is important, that defines who you are?"

Caroline thought a moment. "No. My life's very uneventful."

"Did anything unusual happen at the time of your birth? Did a crow land near your mother's birthing tent? Did clouds cover the sun at that moment? Did a horse kick a dog? Did flowers suddenly bloom?"

"How could I know if any of those things happened when I was born? I was just an infant."

"Your mother and your grandmother and all the old ones of your village would tell you about it over and over. Every child knows why he is named."

Caroline sighed. "I see what you mean. Well, my mother died when I was born."

Crooked Feather's face softened. "I am

sorry. I lost my parents when I was a child."

"Then you're an orphan."

Crooked Feather cocked his head to one side, frowning.

"What is an orphan?"

"A child who has no one to care for it because its parents are dead."

"I had many people to care for me. My mother's sisters and brothers raised me as if I were one of their own children. Among my people it makes no difference if you lose your parents. Someone in the village will raise you. Is that not the way it was with you?"

Caroline looked at the ground, thinking about Aunt Oriona's hatred and her father's constant absence.

"Never mind," she said softly. "Oh—I just remembered something unusual that happened on the night I was born. It was raining very hard, a terrible rainstorm. The bridge washed away. Does that count toward a name?"

Crooked Feather smiled. "Rain is a good omen. It is sent by the Great Spirit to make the grass green for the buffalo and to fill the rivers and streams."

"Aunt Oriona said being born in a storm

brings bad luck. She said it means the devil is beating his wife, and a child born on that day will be wicked. I love the rain. Seems like everything important in my life happens when it's raining."

"A name will come to you. Be patient," Crooked Feather said as he rose to his feet. "Things do not always come easy. I have been waiting years for a vision to come to me so I will know which animal is my protector." He sighed and slung a bow over one shoulder.

Caroline was not yet ready to say good-bye, so she tagged along beside him as he walked toward an open field where tepees had been set up in neat rows. Smoke gently curled up from each top, and women and children were busily working at chores.

"You speak English very well, Crooked Feather," Caroline said in her most pleasant voice. "Where did you learn?"

"Boarding school," he replied.

"Your family sent you away to boarding school?"

He snorted and chuckled lightly.

"Did I say something wrong?" Caroline asked cautiously.

"The last thing my family wanted was for me to attend White Man's school. I left kicking and screaming and tried to run away every night for the first month."

"Then why did you go?"

"The government wanted to civilize me. To make me forget my savage ways, learn to read and write like a white boy."

"But there's nothing wrong with going to school. You should be grateful for receiving a good education."

Crooked Feather put his hands on his hips and laughed so hard people stared at him.

"Why are you laughing?" Caroline tried to hide the annoyance in her voice, but it was getting more difficult with each passing moment.

"Because if I don't laugh, then I shall surely cry," Crooked Feather said at last, after catching his breath. He gave a polite bow. "If you'll excuse me now, miss, I must return to my work. There is another performance this afternoon." He paused. "Are you coming to the second show?"

"I don't have any more money. All I have of value is this pearl button."

"Is this the first Wild West show you've ever seen?"

Caroline nodded. "Yes, it is, but my mother was a performer in Shawnee Sam's show fourteen years ago."

"Your mother?" His eyes grew large and round. "What act did she perform?"

"She rode on a beautiful white horse that danced. I suppose she was a trick rider."

"What was her name?"

"They called her Princess Dancing Rain, but I don't know if she was a real princess."

Crooked Feather's amazement grew. "She was Indian? That would explain your courage with the rattlesnake and your ability to talk to the animals."

"Did you know her?" Caroline felt her excitement grow.

"Sorry, but that was before my time. Fourteen years ago I was hardly out of my mother's cradleboard. Who were her people?"

"What do you mean?"

"Was she Sioux? Crow? Cheyenne?"

"I don't know. No one knows."

"Do you have anything that belonged to her?"

"A neckband with little colored beads all over it. And I have an old show poster."

"Bring the neckband this afternoon, and I

may be able to tell you who her people were."

"But I don't have any money to get back into the show."

"Give me your hand."

Crooked Feather rubbed a moistened finger into his face paint, then made a design of a red feather on Caroline's hand.

"Show this to the gatekeeper, and he will let you in."

Caroline said good-bye and thank you to Crooked Feather, then hurried home. All the while she walked, she held her hand out in front of her, staring at the red marks.

When she arrived at the boardinghouse, she had to dodge Mrs. Carraway, who was arguing with Mattie. Caroline sneaked up the stairs, changed her clothes, then returned and pretended to have been upstairs all along, but the two women did not believe her. Mattie promptly commanded her cousin to wash off the red feather, then sent her to her room in shame, saying, "You shall never be allowed out alone, Miss Caroline Long."

That afternoon Mattie was busy helping Mrs. Carraway prepare for an afternoon tea party featuring as guest of honor Bubbles the cat. Mrs. Carraway had recently stitched a lovely needlepoint cushion, flowers on one side, black velvet on the reverse. Mattie prepared a bowl of white chalk. Bubbles, if in a cooperative mood, would dip her dainty paw in the chalk and "paint" the black velvet, leaving prints and patterns to be examined and interpreted by one Madame Yolinda, who also gave readings of tea leaves and palms.

Though Caroline would have loved to see Bubbles paint, she knew now was the perfect time to slip out unnoticed. Ignoring Mattie's orders to wash her hand, Caroline took the colorful beaded neckband and the poster from her hope chest, and crept out the side door while Mattie and Mrs. Carraway tinkered in the kitchen, making lemon tea cakes.

Thirty minutes later, hot, tired, and out of breath, Caroline stood in front of the fairgrounds' ticket booth, holding her painted hand out to the gatekeeper.

Caroline knew that someone in the show had information about her mother. She could feel the vibrations of the past with every beat of the drum that was pounding in one of the tepees. It was only a matter of hours, perhaps minutes, until she would learn the truth about her mother. Maybe one of her relatives was in this very show. Caroline took a deep breath as she approached the grandstand, knowing that what she was about to do could very well change her life forever.

7

Caroline was even more enthralled with the second performance of the day, seeing things she had not noticed before and watching Crooked Feather more closely. This time when he held the snake above his head and danced, her heart raced in rhythm with the tom-toms.

Since it was the show's final performance in Saint Louis, the attendance that afternoon was the greatest. After the show, Caroline found herself being pressed on all sides by the hordes of impatient people trying to get to the corrals and the sideshows and the autographing performers before the show left town.

The weather was unseasonably hot and dry. Very little rain had fallen since Caroline's arrival more than a month ago, and sweat trickled down the faces, necks, and backs of the roustabouts, who wasted no time in knocking down the canopy tents and wooden stands. A tormenting dust storm had suddenly whipped up, making their job all the more difficult. In designated pens, the bison, deer, horses, and a few Texas longhorns stirred about restlessly, sending dust over the clothes of the spectators.

Caroline saw Crooked Feather helping his uncles push and prod the resistant buffalo into one of the railroad cars that ran on an offshoot of the main track alongside the fairgrounds. The buffalo balked and bellowed and snorted, causing nearby mules to bray, horses to whinny, and chickens to cackle. All this mingled with the snapping and popping of the canvas tents and the scattering of programs, papers, and hats across the fairgrounds. Caroline had never heard the likes of it before, and so great was the noise and confusion that she was not noticed by anyone.

The stars of the show had little hand in the manual work. Instead they signed autographs for the last time, posed for a photographer, or visited the temporary saloons set up in tents across the railroad tracks.

For the price of a dime, the old Indian chiefs, still in full headdresses, put their marks on programs or colorful promotional couriers that had been passed out at local businesses.

Caroline felt very foolish caught up in the midst of the melee, and seeing that Crooked Feather was too busy to speak to her, she decided to study the older Indians, who stood aloofly apart from the younger ones. Their faces wore their histories like words carved into stone. Deep lines; dark, lost eyes; and calm dignity distinguished them from the younger men, who smiled and joked among themselves and appeared to love the attention.

Caroline hesitantly spoke to one of the chiefs, then another. But they ignored her, giving her stiff blue muslin skirt, crisp white blouse, and side-buttoned gaiters no more than a casual glance. However, when she reached into her bag and removed the elaborate beadwork neckband, all eyes followed her. One of the old men smiled and spoke to the man next to him. They nodded and carried on a conversation in their calm and beautiful language, with each word spoken slowly, clearly, and with feeling. Caroline cleared her throat and stepped closer to the Indian who seemed the most friendly and most talkative.

"Excuse me, sir. Have you seen this neckband before? It belonged to my mother, an Indian princess who rode with this Wild West show fourteen years ago."

The men grew silent. Caroline looked from one emotionless face to the next but saw no light of recognition.

"Doesn't anyone here speak English?" she asked.

"Even if they did, they would not talk to you," a voice said behind her. Caroline turned around and saw Crooked Feather, sweat dripping from his temples.

Caroline sighed with relief. "I brought my mother's neckband. Can you tell me what tribe she was with?"

"Tribe?" Crooked Feather snorted but didn't say anything as he took the beadwork in his hands and turned it over and over.

"It doesn't look Sioux, and it isn't Crow or Blackfoot. I have a feeling it's Pawnee or Osage, maybe Wichita. Let me ask this old Pawnee warrior, Lost Wolf. I learned some Pawnee from my roommate in boarding school, even though we were forbidden to speak Indian languages."

Crooked Feather spoke softly and respectfully to an old man, the oldest of them all, sitting on a barrel, dozing off to sleep. Caroline wondered how it was possible that he was able to withstand the long train rides, and the dancing performances, and the riding and whooping. His headdress was the longest of any, cascading to the ground, dwarfing his small, frail body.

Using sign language when words failed, Crooked Feather showed the old man the neck-piece, pointing to Caroline once. A few minutes later, he returned, smiling.

"Just as I thought. It's Wichita, maybe Waco. Lost Wolf says it's very old and crafted by a master, probably an old woman who made it for your mother as a gift."

"Has he seen it before? Does he remember my mother? I brought the poster." She unrolled the faded sheet of thick paper. "Maybe he knew her?"

Crooked Feather studied it closely. "I'll

show it to the old chiefs. Maybe one of them remembers, but most of them were not with the show fourteen years ago."

Caroline twitched and twisted as Crooked Feather showed the poster first to Lost Wolf, then to the others. As they spoke among themselves, some of them laughed, and others shook their heads. One of them waved it away, made secret signs over it, then spit at it as if it were a ghost.

"Why did he do that?" Caroline asked Crooked Feather, removing the spittle with her gloved hand.

"His people don't care much for pictures of dead folks."

"Who is he?"

"His name means Big Tree. Shawnee Sam calls him Billy Big Tree."

"I remember him; he performed a rain dance. Did you tell Big Tree that my mother was dead?"

Crooked Feather stared at Caroline blankly a moment, then his eyebrows rose higher as her words sank in.

"No, I did not mention that the woman in the picture was dead."

"Then why would Big Tree spit on her?"

"You pose an interesting question. As I think of it more, he is a Wichita himself."

As Caroline studied the old man, she remembered that he was the one in the parade who stared at her as he walked by. Of all the old chiefs there, his eyes seemed the blackest and the most intimidating. The tattoos on his face and hands were frightening, but Caroline swallowed her fear and walked closer to him. She looked at his face, then glanced at the face in the reproduction, trying to see similarities. But the poster was not a real photograph. It was a faded artistic rendition, with all the features dramatized. Caroline was not even sure that the woman depicted was a real person.

"Do you know this woman?" she asked the old man and held the poster in front of his startled eyes. He was short, not even as tall as Caroline.

He made the strange signs in the air again and turned his back and walked away. Caroline wanted to follow him, but Crooked Feather grabbed her elbow.

"Not now. Big Tree doesn't want to be disturbed. You can't just thrust the picture of a dead person in his face and expect him to start talking. You have to be respectful and subtle. It takes time."

"But I don't have time. The show is packing up to leave now, and I may never see Big Tree again."

Crooked Feather shrugged lightly. "Our next stop is Indianapolis. Come visit the show there." He smiled and pointed to Caroline's hat, a floppy tam-o'-shanter. "Pretty hat. Remember to keep away from the mules next time."

He glanced in the direction of the train, where roustabouts were securing the gold wagons, the stagecoach, and pieces of equipment onto flatbed cars. The cowboys and vaqueros loaded the mules, longhorns, and horses into wooden cattle cars, whistling and whooping and twirling ropes.

"I have to leave now to help my uncles," Crooked Feather said. "Good luck with your quest." He made a sign with his right hand, holding up two fingers.

"What does that mean? 'Crazy girl'?"

He smiled. "It means 'Go in peace, friend.' "

Caroline made the sign herself.

As Caroline watched Crooked Feather trot to the train, her heart sank to her feet. The old chiefs, after losing interest in her and her neck-band, had turned their backs and returned to the field to watch the women dismantling the tepees.

The dust storm continued, whipping scraps of paper—old tickets, programs, and hand-bills—across the fairgrounds. The roustabouts worked at a frantic pace, fighting the canvas tents that whipped in the strong breeze. From the saloon, the laughter of sharpshooters, trick riders, and sundry performers drifted into the air. Shawnee Sam himself staggered out holding a whiskey bottle.

Caroline watched the Indian women busily knocking down tepees without any help from the Indian men, who had by now settled in the last car of the train. Through the opened doors and windows, she saw them huddled in circles, playing card games. The one they called Big Tree sat apart from the others in the open door, a blanket wrapped around his narrow shoulders. He looked so lonely and sad, Caroline's heart ached for him, even though he had been rude to her.

Lightning streaked across the sky, and almost at the same time thunder shattered the evening air. Caroline shuddered and hugged her body.

When she turned around for one final look, she saw Billy Big Tree standing in the door, his arms outstretched toward the sky. As he lifted his voice in an eerie chant, a light rain began to fall. Caroline stared at him, and for a brief instant their eyes met. Then he pulled his blanket over his head and vanished back inside the train.

Caroline slowly walked around the fairgrounds, thankful that the rain had stopped almost as soon as it had started. But the air was cool now, and the evening sky was dark. Already the shops were closed and the lamplighter was making his rounds up and down the main streets of town. By tomorrow morning Shawnee Sam's Wild West Extravaganza would be gone and along with it her hopes of ever finding out the truth about her mother. Caroline prayed that Crooked Feather or someone would come back out and speak to her again, but soon the animals were loaded and most of the roustabouts had gone to the saloons for a final drink.

With a sigh, Caroline slowly walked back to the boardinghouse. She knew she would receive a tongue-lashing for being out, but she did not care. When she arrived, she saw a carriage in front of the house and imagined that some old crow of a woman was still there admiring Bubbles's pawprints and trying to read the future. Maybe it was Madame Yolinda herself.

Caroline gently opened the front door and tiptoed to the staircase unnoticed. The sound of a familiar voice made her halt in the foyer.

"Father!" Caroline gasped softly.

Her first instinct was to run into the parlor and throw her arms around Andrew Jackson Long, but part of her heart remembered the last time she had seen him. He had been selling her beloved horse, Bellissimo, to a stranger and putting her on a train to Saint Louis.

Caroline slipped to the hall tree and hid behind his greatcoat. It smelled of tobacco and wine and leather. Her heart beat faster and her fingers trembled as she listened to a lively conversation on the verge of boiling over into a raging argument.

"Well, I must say, you've outdone yourself this time, Jackson." Cousin Mattie's voice rang with indignant anger. "Child nabbing your own daughter and holding her for ransom. I didn't think that even *you* would stoop that low."

"Cousin Mattie, how can you use such harsh words? It wasn't intentional child nabbing. You said yourself that you pitied Caroline for having to live with Aunt Oriona, and you willingly agreed to let her stay here until I returned."

"I didn't know it would be so long, Jackson. I'm not rich, you know. I've a very limited income. She's a sweet child, but still, expenses are expenses. I've had to curtail many of my favorite activities on her behalf."

Caroline felt a sharp lump rise to her throat. She thought Mattie enjoyed her company.

"I'll gladly give you some of the money Oriona gives me to cover your confounded expenses."

"Here, now, I'll thank you to watch your unseemly language, sir. There are ladies and children in this house," Mrs. Carraway's Irish brogue interrupted.

"Of course. A thousand pardons, madame."

As Caroline fought back tears of anger, she heard a familiar impatient *rap-tap-tap* on the hardwood floor. A cold chill swept over Caroline as Aunt Oriona's high-pitched voice, annoyed and angry as usual, rang out.

"Stop the foolish bickering, Jackson and Mattie. Just fetch Caroline and pack her belongings so we can be off."

"Tell me, Oriona, just how much did you pay Jackson for the privilege of learning where Caroline was staying?" The irritation bristled in Mattie's voice and Caroline imagined her planting her hands on her hips.

"Don't answer that, Aunt Oriona," Jackson interrupted.

"Not that it's your business, Mattie, but the figure was ten thousand dollars," Oriona said with a sniff. "And well worth it for Jackson to agree to get out of Caroline's life and never return."

"If you believe that, Stepmother, then you are an old fool," Mattie hissed.

"Not so much the fool this time. The solicitor drew up the formal adoption papers, and Jackson will sign them before receiving a penny."

"I'm growing impatient, Mattie. Where is Caroline?" Jackson's voice bellowed and he rushed up the stairs, sweeping past the trembling greatcoat hanging in the foyer.

Caroline heard him opening doors, and the screams of women. Mattie followed him in a swirl of crackling petticoats and crisp cotton chintz skirt. She faced him at the bottom of the stairwell, a few feet from the coatrack.

"So this was your scheme all along?" she whispered. "I took care of the child for two months, without a penny's support from you. And now you are going to collect a fortune for *my* troubles. It isn't fair!"

"Where is she?" Jackson demanded. But Mattie stood her ground.

"You owe me, cousin. Heaven knows, I'll never get a penny out of the old bat any other way. In all the years I lived with her and Papa, she never showed me the slightest affection. I know I won't receive a dime's worth of inheritance when she dies. Especially now that she's adopting Caroline."

"All right, all right," Jackson said, interrupting her. "I'll give you five hundred dollars. That's well worth more than you deserve."

"Two thousand dollars and not a penny less. I've just had the most exhilirating idea come to me. I should absolutely *love* to purchase a motorcar. Wouldn't it be grand to be the first woman in Saint Louis to own one? I would become the talk of the town."

"You're a blood-sucking vampire, worthy of Oriona's name." Jackson spewed out curses, then with a heavy sigh, he waved his hands. "Very well, I'll give you two thousand dollars."

"Today, the very moment Oriona hands it to you."

Another barrage of curses filled the foyer. "Very well, you shrew. Where is Caroline?"

"This way. I sent her to her room earlier this afternoon. She must be sound asleep."

Caroline watched the two hurrying toward Mattie's room. As they entered the bedroom, Caroline bolted out the front door and ran down the steps. She picked up her skirt and ran with all her might toward the railroad tracks. She heard the whistle of the show train as it slowly pulled away from the fairgrounds. The train would pass only two blocks from the boardinghouse as it made a gentle curve and then headed over the river bridge. Caroline raced like the wind until at last she saw the trestle. The chug of the engine grew louder as it picked up steam.

Caroline ran with all her strength until at last, exhausted and out of breath, she climbed up on a small wooden platform near the bridge and watched the steam roll from under the wheels of the approaching train. The lanterns swung from the sides, casting yellow light across the tracks.

Caroline waited and waited as the cars passed by. Some were covered passenger cars, some were flatbeds with equipment, others were open livestock cars. Several times she started to jump, but her legs would not cooperate. When she saw the end of the train approaching, her breath came faster. It was now or never. Only one open car was left. With a prayer on her lips, Caroline jumped.

She rolled, then slammed into the opposite wall. Stars flashed behind her eyes, and the last thing she sensed before passing out was the smell of straw and manure.

8

Something moved across Caroline's cheek. Something wet and warm. She opened her eyes and stared into the yellow eyes of an Angora goat. It sniffed Caroline's hair, then licked her cheek again with its tongue.

"Thanks for waking me up," Caroline said with a chuckle. As she gently pushed the goat away, pain shot through her left shoulder. She rubbed it absentmindedly while she studied the insides of the train car. She had landed on a pile of hay and was surrounded by sheep and goats.

The night air had grown cool, so Caroline crawled closer to a woolly sheep and pulled some straw up to her chin. She snuggled in the hay, staring up at the brilliant stars. She tried not to think of her father's betrayal, but tears filled her eyes and she sobbed until the monotonous *click-clack* of the train lulled her to sleep.

Caroline woke to the sound of squealing brakes. Bright sunlight streamed in through the uncovered car and through the cracks in the wooden slats, bathing her stiff body in delicious warmth. She sat up, scattering piles of straw around her like a yellow blanket. For a few moments she clasped her arms around her knees. Her head ached, her stomach roared with hunger, and the stench of manure was making her nauseous.

"What have I gotten myself into?" she whispered aloud as she rubbed her sore shoulder. "I must have been insane last night."

The creaking of the train wheels grew louder, and billows of steam drifted past the car as the train slowed and at last halted.

Caroline peeked out the slats. On one side of the train she saw farms dotted with dairy cows and crops of corn or wheat. On the other side she saw a distant city, its smokestacks billowing thick gray fumes. A few sparse buildings and some wooden bleachers indicated that they were at fairground facilities. The train clicked and banged and bumped as it backed onto an offshoot of the main track.

A flock of crows in the slick branches of a dead tree cawed loudly.

"Shut up, you stupid varmints! A man can't get a decent night's sleep for your loud mouths." An angry voice rose from somewhere down the line of cars. Suddenly a loud shot cracked through the air. A tree branch shattered into pieces and dropped to the ground, making the crows scream in anger and fly away.

Laughter from the car next door filled the air, and Caroline was reminded of her whereabouts. No doubt she would be in the utmost trouble when discovered, and surely she would be sent back to Saint Louis. Or perhaps she would be taken for a penniless street urchin and sent to an orphanage. Caroline felt foolish and wished she had never begun this adventure.

She heard approaching footsteps and scurried behind the sheep. First she heard voices speaking an Indian language, then the voices of the roustabouts as they opened doors and began pulling down equipment to set up tents, bleachers, and animal pens.

It would only be a matter of time before

Caroline was discovered, if she didn't act now. She peeked through the cracks again and watched the roustabouts stomping their feet and setting up the cook station. Big fifty-gallon metal drums were fixed to metal braces, and firewood was placed under them. Two greasy-looking men bustled about, starting fires and getting out pots and pans and utensils. Soon the strong aroma of coffee permeated every inch of the train car. The roustabouts stood around the fires, sipping coffee, joking, and eating corn pone. Seeing it reminded Caroline of Ester's delicious johnnycakes and made her mouth water.

In an empty field next to the fairgrounds, a group of Indian boys on horses were playing games. The Indian women lugged long cedar tepee poles to the field and began lifting them up into cone shapes and securing them with rawhide strips. Soon more people began to mill about, carrying things off the train and stopping at the cook camp to get tin cups of coffee.

Caroline decided that as soon as a few more people were moving about, she would blend in easily and never be noticed. She sat beside the door, waiting for the best opportunity. It came as the Indian youths returned from the field, leading their ponies past the car, talking and laughing among themselves. Caroline saw Crooked Feather tossing pebbles at another boy. His face was hardly recognizable to her without its red, white, and yellow paint.

"*Psst!* Crooked Feather!" Caroline whispered as loudly as she dared.

He stopped and looked first in the cottonwood tree, then on the roof of the train.

"*Psst!* Over here!"

Crooked Feather swung around, and on seeing Caroline's eyes peering through the slats and her gloved hand waving, his dark eyes exploded with amusement. He glanced to either side, then calmly strolled toward the livestock car. He uprooted a handful of green grass from the side of the railroad tracks and fed it through the slats to a goat.

"What are you doing here?"

"I've run away from my cousin, Mattie. I've come to find out the truth about my mother. That old man, Billy Big Tree, knows something. He might even be related to me. Perhaps my mother's side of the family will welcome me and love me like a prodigal child come home. My father and Cousin Mattie certainly don't care about me." It hurt to say the words, and Caroline's throat grew tight just thinking about the last conversation she had overheard between Mattie and her father.

Crooked Feather opened the door wide enough for Caroline to slip through, and he helped her down. It felt funny to have solid earth beneath her feet at last, and her legs were wobbly.

Crooked Feather glanced inside the car and retrieved Caroline's handbag and the old poster before closing the door.

"I don't see any luggage. Don't you have a plainer dress than the one you're wearing? If you stand around dressed in fancy clothes like that, everyone will take notice and ask questions."

Caroline looked down at her blue muslin skirt, white blouse, and matching blue stockings, all wrinkled and stained from a night in the company of livestock. How could he think these rags were fancy?

"What do you suggest I wear?" Caroline asked.

"With a plain dress made of calico or gingham and a split bonnet, you could pass as one of the pioneer children."

"A split bonnet? I wouldn't be caught dead in one of those awful things. I have a lovely new tam-o'-shanter hat somewhere in that pile of hay." She glanced over her shoulder at the cattle car.

"I imagine the goats had it for breakfast."

Voices drifted over to the train car, and Crooked Feather grabbed Caroline's arm.

"Come with me. I know a place you can hide."

He led Caroline, rather roughly, she thought, to the open fairgrounds, where the Indian women were stretching tanned buffalo skins over the cedar tepee posts. Sacred markings and simple drawings of animals decorated the outsides of some of the skins.

Crooked Feather spoke to a woman whose arms were loaded with a thick brown buffalo hide. She remained silent all the while she listened, her black eyes focused on Caroline.

Caroline could not tell if there was fear or hatred or amusement in the woman's calm face, but after Crooked Feather finished speaking, the woman nodded and slipped inside the nearest tepee. She returned in a moment with a folded bundle of buckskin in her arms.

Crooked Feather thanked her and pushed the bundle into Caroline's arms. "Change into these. With your dark hair and eyes, you can pass for one of the Indian girls."

"I'll do no such thing," Caroline protested with indignation. "Why, those clothes will make me look awful. I won't do it."

"If you do not want my advice, so be it. You'll be caught and returned to your relatives in Saint Louis." Crooked Feather pivoted and started walking toward the woman who had given him the clothes.

"Wait!" Caroline shouted, and trotted after him. "I'll put on those smelly old things. But will you help me find my mother's relatives?"

"Agreed." He held the flaps of the tepee open. "Change clothes in here."

When Caroline stepped inside the tepee, her head swirled with strange sensations. The enclosure smelled of tanned buffalo skins and smoke flowing out an open flap at the top of the tepee. The woman who had given Caroline the clothes squatted near the crackling fire, preparing food. A younger woman with a papoose strapped to her back ground corn on a large gray stone. Two children played on buffalo hides spread on the floor.

There was no privacy, so Caroline changed clothes with the two children staring at her unmentionables and giggling as they pointed at her blue stockings and white petticoat. The women continued to work but kept glancing at the stranger from the corners of their eyes, whispering and snickering.

The buckskin tunic and leggings felt thick yet soft, and the smell reminded Caroline of Bellissimo's leather reins and saddle. As an afterthought, she removed the beaded neckband from her crocheted handbag and fastened it around her neck.

The younger woman smiled timidly and pointed to Caroline's curly black hair, then at her own long braids.

"Ah, you want to braid my hair?" Caroline asked.

The woman nodded.

Her slender brown fingers felt gentle as she rapidly twisted strands over and under, over and under, to make a tight braid on each side of Caroline's head. The women and children broke into giggles. Caroline longed for a mirror to look at herself in, but on second thought decided perhaps it would be better if she didn't know what she looked like.

Quickly she pulled back the tent flaps and emerged, the two children following close behind, tugging at the long fringes hanging down from the buckskin tunic.

Crooked Feather pushed away from the brown-and-white spotted horse he had been leaning against.

"Caroline?" he asked.

"Don't say a word or I shall go jump in the river. Oh, these clothes feel so strange, but I suppose I shall get used to them eventually. There is an unusual hole in the sleeve here." Caroline stuck her finger in the hole. "Whatever caused this?"

Crooked Feather hesitated, then shrugged.

"You will no doubt find out sooner or later—it's a bullet hole."

"What does it mean?"

Crooked Feather shifted his weight uncomfortably and glanced over his shoulders. He put his hand on Caroline's back and steered her away from the tepees to the area where the cowboys were building temporary corrals.

"It doesn't mean anything important. You look like a real Indian *princess,*" he said jokingly. "No white man will be able to tell the difference. Shawnee Sam will think you're one of Standing Horse's daughters. You can stay here with his wife, Afraid-of-Birds."

"I don't have any money to pay for my room and board," Caroline said sadly.

"Afraid-of-Birds would not think of taking money from a guest. But if you help her with chores, like bringing firewood and buckets of water, and small things like that, I'm sure she would appreciate your kindness."

"Chores? I—I've never done chores before. Ester and Taffy did everything for me. Grandmother Long hated for me to do manual work, saying it wasn't ladylike. But I can play the piano, and my needlework is excellent."

Crooked Feather was laughing at her. Caroline saw it clearly in his twinkling eyes and the way he was holding his lips to stop the grin.

"Well, what do you expect?" she insisted, tugging at the buckskin shirt. "I was being groomed to become a fine lady. Besides, I'm an Indian princess, now. A princess doesn't have to work." She held out her arms and smiled triumphantly.

Crooked Feather snorted.

"Ha! Princess is White Man's notion. Among my people, each chief is chosen for his deeds, valor, and wisdom, not because of who his father was."

"Well, what about the chief's family? Aren't they special?"

"Indeed. His wives and daughters must set an example and be the best at everything. His women must skin hides faster and chase rabbits quicker. They must gather wood more skillfully and beat clothes harder in the river. They must face the enemy with courage. If not, they disgrace the chief."

"Oh," Caroline said, and felt the corners of her lips droop. She glanced up and saw that Crooked Feather's eyes danced with merriment. His laughter rolled from deep in his throat and he slapped his legs.

But his laughter stopped when a tall man in knee-high boots, a snug-fitting fringed buckskin jacket, and a wide-brimmed hat rode by on a beautiful Appaloosa horse. Caroline had seen him in the entry parade in Saint Louis and in the center ring during the Wild West show.

"It's Shawnee Sam," she whispered, then

got very quiet, following Crooked Feather's lead. Crooked Feather held up his hand in a sign of greeting, and Shawnee Sam did the same, saying a few words in Crooked Feather's language.

Suddenly Shawnee Sam swung his horse around. He stared at Caroline with piercing green eyes beneath craggy blond eyebrows.

"This isn't Standing Horse's daughter, is it?" he asked in a deep baritone voice that of itself was enough to frighten a child.

"No," Crooked Feather quickly replied. "She is the granddaughter of one of the old ones."

"Those clothes look familiar. Isn't she wearing the same costume that Standing Horse's daughter was wearing when—"

"Yes," Crooked Feather quickly replied.

"Is she going to take the other girl's place?"

"I—I don't think so—"

"Yes, I am," Caroline quickly finished the sentence. There was no reason why she couldn't do whatever it was that the other girl had done, whoever she was. "I'm very skilled. I am an Indian princess."

Shawnee Sam's eyes lit up like firecrackers

and a grin spread across his lips, half buried by his handlebar mustache and a wavy goatee.

"Indeed. A very pretty Indian princess, too. Can you ride a horse?"

"Absolutely."

"Are you a roughrider?" he asked in a teasing manner.

"Yes, of course." Though Caroline didn't know exactly what she was expected to do, she was confident that Crooked Feather would teach her. After all, she could ride a horse as well as any girl her age. And she did not remember seeing Indian women do anything particularly difficult in the show.

"By the way, where did you learn to speak such good English? I don't detect the slightest accent," Shawnee Sam said as he leaned on his saddle horn.

Caroline felt the air rush from her lungs as if she'd been punched. For several seconds her brain whirled before she knew what to say.

"Boarding school," she replied, proud of her good memory.

"They certainly did an excellent job with you," Shawnee Sam said. "You have none of the submissive manners of some other Indian girls I've seen return from the boarding schools. Which one was it you attended?"

Caroline felt the blood drain from her cheeks. She opened her mouth, hoping something would spill out. Then she heard Crooked Feather clear his throat.

"Was it Carlisle Industrial School?" Crooked Feather asked calmly.

Caroline nodded and let out her breath. "Yes, Carlisle."

"Ah, yes, that explains it." Shawnee Sam smiled. "I've met Captain Pratt several times. You attended Carlisle, too, didn't you, Crooked Feather?"

"Yes, sir, I did."

"Captain Pratt does a fine job of civilizing you people."

"Yes, sir," Crooked Feather replied, his eyes seething with anger. "Captain Pratt does everything in his power to make the Indian forget his tribal ways. I believe his credo is 'Kill the Indian to save the man.'"

Shawnee Sam frowned. "Now, now, I wouldn't put it quite that way."

"No, sir, you wouldn't," Crooked Feather replied.

"Very well, then." Shawnee Sam ignored Crooked Feather and nodded to Caroline. "We'll see how well you do tomorrow with my wife."

"Thank you, Shawnee Sam," Caroline said, and curtsied.

After Sam had ridden off, Caroline and Crooked Feather walked across the field to the tepees. They watched the women working busily to gather firewood, haul water, and cook. Several men were riding on horseback, trying to touch each other with fancy feathered sticks. All the while, Crooked Feather remained silent, deep in his own thoughts, a solemn expression clouding his face.

"What game are those men playing?" Caroline asked at last.

"It isn't a game—they are practicing counting coup. Touching your enemy with a coup stick is an act of bravery, more so than killing him."

"If you want to join them, please do not let me stop you."

Crooked Feather glanced at Caroline. "I do not play games with the older men very often. They do not welcome me."

"Why not? Aren't you as skilled as they are at riding a horse?"

"How can I compare to them? At my age, those men endured the torturous sun dance to gain visions, and they still bear scars of honor. They rode with the great Satanta on glorious horse raids. Now, the sun dance is forbidden, and I will never raid for ponies. Riding was discouraged at boarding school, and of course we never counted coup."

"But you speak English perfectly and understand arithmetic. I imagine your family is very proud of you for being so well educated."

A look of disbelief filled his eyes. "You speak like a white man."

"What do you mean?"

"The day I arrived at boarding school when I was eight years old, my buckskin clothes were ripped off and burned and I was dressed in a cotton-and-denim uniform. Even the medicine bag that protected me from evil spirits was taken away. My hair, which fell down my back in long tresses, was cut and tossed to the floor like trash. My manhood was gone and I wanted to die. Indeed, one of the boys I knew did take his own life, so great was his shame. Not one of the boys did not break down and weep.

"My sisters were put in calico dresses and their hair twisted above their heads and aprons put at their waists. Instead of learning to grind corn and weave baskets, skin hides, and erect tepees, they were taught to sew with needles and thread, to bake bread, and to scrub clothes in washtubs.

"The schoolmasters forced us to eat White Man's food, even though it made us sick. If any of us were caught speaking our native language, we were thrashed and put in isolation or our mouths were washed out with lye soap. At every turn, we were whipped or struck or yelled at like undisciplined cattle.

"The beliefs of my people were forbidden. We were not allowed to pray to the Great Spirit to celebrate the arrival of spring. We were told the great sun dance was cruel and barbaric. We were forced to attend White Man's church, and we memorized scriptures from the Bible, even though we did not understand what they meant. They told us that our tribal gods were evil. We were made to feel that our parents were wicked to have taught us such awful customs.

"They told us that Indians had massacred innocent white men and committed horrible atrocities...Sioux were forced to sit next to their old enemies, and Crow sat next to Comanches. I shared a bunk bed with a Pawnee, whom my people detested for being farmers. We were all one and the same in the eyes of the white schoolmasters."

Caroline shifted her weight uncomfortably. "I'm sorry you were so unhappy, Crooked Feather. When you graduated from school, did you return to the reservation? Was your family glad to have you back?"

Crooked Feather clenched his jaw.

"We returned to our families, but we no longer belonged. We'd grown up at the boarding schools and did not learn the sacred rituals of our people. Indeed, when we first came back, we laughed at the old ways and showed no respect for our elders. We spit out their foods and complained about sleeping on buffalo robes instead of soft beds. We said bad things to the faces of our mothers and fathers and old uncles. We called them ignorant and superstitious.

And when the old ones saw that their children were no longer theirs, they wept and cast us out. They called us the Lost People."

"Is that why you are here in the Wild West show?"

He nodded. "Here I can dress and act like an Indian, and white men think I am Indian. But the old ones know better."

A long silence fell over Crooked Feather, and Caroline saw his eyes fill with pain. She wanted to touch his shoulder but was afraid he would think it the act of a white woman. She decided that the best thing to do was to change the subject. She cleared her throat.

"Well, what do you think of Shawnee Sam wanting me to be in the program tomorrow? Only one day here and already I've secured a position. How thrilling!"

But Crooked Feather's eyes did not share Caroline's enthusiasm.

"What is wrong?" she asked as an uneasy feeling crept over her.

"He wants you to be in the program with his wife, Sure Shot Sue."

"Is that so bad? I saw her the last day of the show in Saint Louis. She was rather exciting, I thought."

"Exciting? That depends on where you are standing."

"What do you mean?"

"Let me explain it to you by pointing out that the hole in the sleeve of that buckskin dress is a bullet hole. It was put there by Sure Shot Sue last week. The girl who was wearing the dress now has a hole in her arm and cannot ride or do anything useful. She was sent back to Indian Territory by Shawnee Sam."

"She was Standing Horse's daughter?"

"Yes."

"But isn't Sure Shot Sue supposed to be a good shot? One of the best, like Annie Oakley or Johnny Baker?"

Crooked Feather laughed. "Her name should not even be mentioned in the same breath as theirs. Sue was good in her day, but she likes to nip the bottle to steady her nerves before a show. Lately she does more than nip, and it does more than steady her nerves; it destroys them altogether. Last week wasn't the first time she shot someone, but if it is just an Indian, no one cares. I'm waiting for the day when she wings someone in the audience—then we'll hear about it."

Caroline swallowed hard. "And I'm

supposed to help Sue tomorrow? What do I have to do?"

"You are the one who will hold up an ear of corn to be shot out of your hand."

Caroline felt sick.

"I've changed my mind. I don't want to do it."

"You would go back on a promise?" Crooked Feather's face registered his disgust.

"No." She sighed. "I guess not."

"If you survive, you must try to find another position in the show."

"Yes," Caroline said weakly, still stunned at her bad luck.

"I can put you on a beautiful pinto, put feathers in your hair, and teach you a few tricks. Maybe you can convince Shawnee Sam that you can ride well enough to take part in the trick-riding event."

"That sounds wonderful," Caroline said, trying to sound enthusiastic, "but first I have to survive Sure Shot Sue."

9

The wife of Standing Horse had taken the name Afraid-of-Birds because when she was a child a flock of startled doves flew in her face and for many years after that the sight of birds had frightened her. Though she was middle-aged now and no longer afraid of birds, and in fact liked them immensely, she kept the name because it had brought her good luck throughout her life.

Afraid-of-Birds took Caroline into her tepee without a grumble or complaint. Though she did not speak much English, she communicated with her new lodger using gestures and facial expressions that made the children laugh. Her smile, emphasized by small teeth worn down by years of chewing skins, and her small puggish nose and twinkling black eyes gave her the look of an impish pixie.

Afraid-of-Birds gave Caroline a pair of beautifully beaded moccasins and some feathers for her hair. In return Caroline gave the generous woman her white petticoat and blue cotton stockings. Afraid-of-Birds immediately and gleefully pulled the petticoat over her buckskin skirt and did a little dance of joy, making her children and sister roll with laughter. Then, with Caroline's directions, she pulled the stockings onto her sturdy legs.

It was a sight to see, and Caroline bit her lip to keep from laughing with the children, but Afraid-of-Birds ignored them all and proudly walked out of the tent and up and down the open field, pretending she needed to gather wood. Others laughed at her and pointed and made remarks, but the hardy woman could not be intimidated and returned with her arms full of firewood and a grin on her face.

Later that morning, when Caroline finally found a bit of mirror, she was amazed at her transformation. In the buckskin clothing and with her hair woven into braids, she was sure she would be accepted on any reservation in the country. And she was amazed how much she resembled the woman in the poster, which was now resting in the corner of the tepee.

Caroline strolled the grounds, watching the roustabouts set up canopies, ticket stands, and bleachers for the main arena. No one paid her the least bit of attention, which suited her fine, because she had never laid eyes on a more un-kempt and unruly group of men in her whole life. In old stinky clothes, the roustabouts swung heavy sledgehammers, pounding poles into hard ground that was in need of a good rain. The men cursed in a way that would burn the ears of any decent girl, infuriating Caroline.

"Sir, please watch your language in the presence of a young lady," she said to one particularly repugnant man, repeating the words she had heard her cousin, Mattie, say to many a crusty man.

"Young lady?" The man stopped swinging his sledgehammer and shot a stream of disgusting tobacco juice, half of which lodged in his bushy black beard. "Where?" He roared with laughter, and likewise his smelly companions chuckled.

"Get out of here, Injun," said another man, rudely poking Caroline with the end of his shovel. "Get back to your tepee."

"I am not an Indian," Caroline insisted. "I am Caroline Elizabeth Long. How dare you speak to me in such a tone!" She put her hands on her hips. "I'm only dressed this way for the program."

"Well, well, we got us an educated Injun here. She's been to boarding school and learnt White Man's ways. But I reckon if it has hair like an Injun's"—his filthy fingers touched her braids—"and it has skin like an Injun's"—his fingers touched her face—"and it dresses like an Injun"—his arrogant fingers tugged the fringe of her buckskin jacket—"then it must be an Injun. Now get out of my way." He pushed Caroline so hard she fell to the ground. The men laughed, and no one made a move to help her up.

Caroline felt hot tears fill her eyes but refused to give the bullies the satisfaction of seeing her cry. She picked herself up and brushed off the dust.

"I shall report you to Shawnee Sam, sirs. Each and every one of you." She pointed her fingers first at one, then the others. They did not take her words very lightly, and by the redness of their faces and the bulging of their eyes, Caroline decided that discretion was the better part of valor. She ran toward the corral where some Indians were tending the buffalo.

As Caroline leaned on a post rail and tried to pet one of the dark, curly buffalo heads, one of the Indians said something to her in his language. She stared blankly. He repeated the words, not in an angry tone but in a tone that implied authority. Caroline swallowed hard and wondered what he wanted her to do.

After repeating his words a third time, he studied Caroline more closely, then waved a friend over. Both of them spoke to her, and when she gave no response, they spoke to themselves, as if discussing some great mystery. They touched her hair and turned her head sideways. Then with a snort one of them said to her face, "You not Indian. Go." He pointed a finger to the opposite side of the camp, then turned away and resumed his chores.

Caroline sighed and walked toward the

cook camp, where a few greasy men were chopping potatoes and puting them into the fifty-gallon metal drums. The smell of boiling vegetables and meat filled the air, reminding Caroline that she had not eaten since yesterday. She longed for fresh buckwheat griddlecakes and Towle's Log Cabin maple syrup. The cook, his apron stained brown, tossed her a cold biscuit as if she were a stray dog, but without Ester's apple butter, it tasted bland.

By late morning the fairgrounds crackled with activity. Roughriders practiced fancy riding tricks such as flip-flopping in and out of the saddle, sitting backward, hanging upside down, and scooping up items from the ground as the horses raced in furious haste. Mexican vaqueros twirled lariats in the most fascinating maneuvers, over and under and all around, even tying knots with the twist of a wrist. Caroline was sure that the lead vaquero would be able to spell out his name in the air with his rope.

In a far corner, the champion wing shots practiced shooting round glass balls or clay pigeons tossed in the air. Sure Shot Sue was nowhere to be seen, and that worried Caroline. She imagined Sue under some bar table, intoxicated to the point of stupor. Just the sound of rifles and six-shooters cracking and popping all around made Caroline's stomach jittery.

Up on the bandstand, the musicians practiced tunes, some exciting and daring, others lighthearted and fun. Caroline turned over an old bucket and sat on it, chin resting in hands.

She was deep in thought, imagining which programs went with which tunes, when she saw the old man who had spit at her mother's poster, the one they called Billy Big Tree. He crossed the arena alone, carrying a small drum in one hand and a buckskin pouch in the other. His slow, elegant gait gave the impression of an old elk that had seen too many winters.

Caroline got up and followed at a discreet distance. He removed several items from the pouch—a pipe, an ear of corn, a bow and arrow, feathers, and a turtle-shell rattle. With great purpose in his stride he made a circle in the dirt, then held the items, one at a time, in different directions, all the while speaking in a singsong voice. Each item had its place on the circle. After this ceremony, he settled down on the ground, cross-legged, and patted out a steady rhythm on the drum, singing all the while. None of the show performers gave him a second look, but a few Indians walked over and began to dance to the beat, a steady, unvarying slow rhythm.

"It is a blessing—a prayer," a familiar voice behind Caroline said.

She glanced over her shoulder and saw Crooked Feather standing with his arms crossed, watching the men.

"A prayer for what?" Caroline asked.

"A prayer for good luck at the show while we are here. A prayer that no one gets harmed. A prayer that the food does not run out."

"Why is he the one who prays? Is he a religious leader?"

"You could say that. He was a powerful singer in his day. He brought the rain many times to his people."

"Just by singing and playing drums and dancing? Surely you don't believe that?"

"He believes it and those Pawnee men believe it. According to my roommate in boarding school, the Wichita and Pawnee have similar beliefs. Many lifetimes ago their ancestors were the same people. But they decided to separate at a fork in the river. The Pawnee traveled north and the Wichita traveled south. At least that is how the legend goes."

"What about you? Do you believe in Big Tree's power?"

"I am not Wichita. But still I respect him. The old ones say he can bring the rain. But I have never seen him do it."

"Do you ever speak to him?"

"He is Wichita; I am Kiowa. Our languages are different, but I learned Pawnee from my roommate and many of those words are similar to Wichita. Big Tree understands me better than I understand him."

"Why does he have those black markings around his eyes and down his face?"

"The Wichita call themselves the Raccoon People. I suppose that animal is sacred to them."

"Why does he have those claw designs on his hands?"

"I believe those are placed there after a boy kills his first bird. Every tattoo on his body represents an important honor in his life. I have heard that Wichita men today do not use tattoos so much because white men discourage it. But Big Tree has lived many winters and I imagine his old body is covered with markings."

"I would like to speak to him," Caroline said softly. "Please introduce me formally."

Crooked Feather didn't reply. He waited until the song had ended on several loud notes and the dancers had left.

On silent feet, Crooked Feather walked to the old man. He spoke a few words, and the old man replied in a soft voice. After Big Tree placed his sacred items back in the pouch, Crooked Feather helped the old man up, speaking all the while.

For a long time the old man did not look at Caroline, but at last he turned. His dark eyes narrowed, as if squinting out the sun, but there was no sun in his eyes. He spoke not to Caroline but to Crooked Feather.

"What did he say?" she asked.

"He wants to know if you are Pawnee."

"Tell him no, my mother was Wichita, like him. This neckband belonged to her." She quickly removed it and held it out. The old man stared at it a long time, but he made no move to touch it. He spoke a few more words, then turned and walked away.

Caroline felt frustration sweep over her. "That is the second time that man has been rude and inconsiderate to me," she protested. "I hope that he is not my relative."

Crooked Feather stared after the old man a minute, then turned to Caroline. "He recognized the neckband, and he recognized you."

"He said that?"

"No, but couldn't you tell? It was in his face and eyes."

"All I saw in his face and eyes was disdain. Maybe I was wrong to seek out my mother's people. I thought they would be happy to find that Dancing Rain had a child."

"Give him more time. He is shocked to see you after all these years. You must earn his respect. You must prove yourself worthy."

A loud clang interrupted Crooked Feather's speech. It rang throughout the fairgrounds, reaching every corner. Caroline assumed it was some kind of fire alarm and quickly followed Crooked Feather and the crowd to the source.

"Grub's ready," the scrawny cook shouted as he vigorously banged a metal triangle.

Soon the noise of the shouting cowboys, cracking rifles, and band grew silent, as performers and workers dropped what they were doing and merged at the chuck wagon. The meal wasn't much more than runny stew and cornbread, but Caroline devoured the food like a starving street urchin.

All afternoon the roustabouts continued setting up the tents and stands and booths. The cowboys practiced roping calves and riding broncos. The Indians practiced shooting arrows and racing their ponies.

Inside the tepee, Caroline watched Afraid-of-Birds repair her husband's clothing. Her nimble brown fingers skillfully sewed glass beads and porcupine quills into intricate patterns. Seeing her stooped over her work with a lantern glowing nearby reminded Caroline of Aunt Oriona stooped over her embroidery. But how different the two women were! While Aunt Oriona always sat in silence in her black dresses, Afraid-of-Birds chattered endlessly with her sister or the children, often taking time to laugh at some joke she had made, or to attend the fire or stir the cooking food. She showed Caroline some of her quilling handiwork—baby moccasins, a cradle, a buffalo robe, and most fantastic of all, a parfleche used as a shield by Standing Horse. When Caroline asked the woman how long it had taken to make the robe, the woman held up five fingers. Whether the fingers stood for days or weeks, months or years, Caroline could not say.

That night, the older Indian men gathered around a campfire, smoking pipes and exchanging tales. Caroline wished she knew what they were saying, because from the expression on the faces of the listeners, the tales must have been as tall and wild as the ones being told by the cowboys sitting around their own campfire at the other end of the field, where occasionally laughter would boom out or someone would break into song, accompanied by a banjo. In yet another section of the field, the vaqueros sang Spanish melodies to the soft strumming of a guitar.

Crooked Feather sat on the outskirts of the circle, listening quietly, deep in thought. Caroline slipped beside him and sat down. "What is that old chief saying?" she whispered.

"He is telling of the time before the White Man came, the time when the buffalo covered the prairies and no man or woman or child went hungry. Now the buffalo are all but gone."

"Is that really true?"

"Yes. Shawnee Sam's own book about his days as a buffalo hunter says that there were fifty million buffalo in 1870; five years later there were only one million left. Today they only number in the hundreds. The White Man's repeating rifle made killing them easy."

"Why did they kill so many?"

"Why do you think?"

"For the meat, I guess."

"The White Man left the meat to rot on the prairies."

"For the hides, then."

"Yes, but many times the hunters left all the dead animals, taking nothing to use. They shot them from the passing trains that did not stop."

Caroline sighed. "Then I guess they shot the helpless buffalo just for the sport. Oh, men can be so beastly sometimes!"

Crooked Feather turned and looked at Caroline.

"There is another reason, the most important reason of all, that white men destroyed the buffalo."

Caroline tilted her head to one side. "If not for food or hides or sport, what other reason could there be? None that I can think of."

"You really don't know, do you?"

Caroline shook her head slowly. "No. Tell me."

Crooked Feather rose to his feet. "If you cannot see it, then I cannot explain it." He brushed past her and disappeared into the darkness.

That night Caroline slept on a buffalo hide for the first time. The smell of the curly brown hair and the scenes of buffalo hunts painted on the tepee skins crept into her dreams. She was a woman warrior on a pinto horse, riding alongside the thundering buffalo herd. Their number was so great they covered the rolling hills and the flat prairie and kicked up dust like a storm. But as she rode, her bow and arrow drawn, the buffalo began to vanish one by one, then hundreds at a time, until there were none left, save a very old and tired cow. The cow stood on a hill, tears staining the dark wool beneath her eyes. Caroline drew her bow and aimed the arrow, but she could not bring herself to let it fly. The cow vanished over the empty hill. When Caroline turned around, she saw the people of the village—walking skeletons with loose skin and sunken eye sockets. As they began to vanish one by one, they held out their bony fingers and tried to grab Caroline. She woke with a shout.

Stepping outside for some fresh air, Caroline saw Crooked Feather sitting under a tree gazing at the stars.

"What is wrong?" he asked her. "A bad dream?"

Caroline swallowed and found her throat dry as sand. "Yes. Now I know why all the buffalo were killed."

Crooked Feather grunted. "Then it was not a bad dream. It was real."

The next morning, after a breakfast of biscuits and sausage and eggs, every cowboy polished his boots, brushed his hat, combed his chaps, and curried his horse. The Indian men painted their horses and their own faces and bodies. The roustabouts hitched up mules to the fancy gold circus wagons, and the band practiced its tunes.

The grand entry into the city was about to begin. In the afternoon the first show of the day would be performed. Already curious children, teenage boys, and a few other local citizens were roaming about the fairgrounds. The ticket booth was set up and the man inside had his money box ready. Across the tracks, tents had been pitched for temporary saloons. Unsavory men with waxed mustaches and women with too much rouge on their faces strutted about, inviting the performers to come inside.

At last a sharp whistle blasted and Shawnee Sam, on his prancing Appaloosa stallion, gave a signal. Red-and-gold wagons, cowboys, Indians, vaqueros, fancy riders, a stagecoach, the pioneer wagon, and hordes more began to file from the fairgrounds to the town. The streets were already lined with citizens waving and shouting.

Caroline walked beside Afraid-of-Birds and her two children. Not long ago Caroline had been on the street, waving and smiling and gawking at the Indians. Today she was on the receiving end. The fingers pointed, the children laughed, and the boys made whooping noises and pretended to have feathers in their hair. One small boy threw a stone that hit Caroline's shoulder.

Caroline felt humiliation and outrage throughout the whole procession. By the time they had returned to the fairgrounds, she was so angry she thought she might prefer to be at Aunt Oriona's house.

While the crowd pushed through the gates and filled the stands, the band played a variety of lively songs. Vendors peddled their wares, and outside the main tents several sideshows had been set up with human oddities for the morbidly curious. Con artists and grifters abounded, trying to deceive citizens out of their money.

As the entertainers lined up at the far end of the hippodrome, preparing to make the grand entry, Caroline felt panic race through her heart.

Why did I ever think I could do this? she thought. *If I hurry, I can run to the tepee, change back into my skirt and blouse, and be gone before anyone misses me.*

She spun around and bumped fully into the short, plump form of Sure Shot Sue. Sue's pleasant baby face had the look of a cherub's, but her snug-fitting buckskin clothes and the rifle casually slung over one shoulder gave her the appearance of a woman not to be crossed.

"Are you the girl taking the place of Standing Horse's daughter?" Sue asked in a very flat, countrified voice.

Caroline nodded.

"Then come with me. I'll show you what to do. We go on right after the grand entry."

Sue took Caroline's elbow with a grip as strong as that of any man. Sue's silk Arabian-style tent, which she shared with Shawnee Sam, was a far cry from the simple tepees and the canvas tents of the other performers. It reeked of whiskey and perfume and the sweet scent of dozens of flowers from admirers.

"All you have to do is hold this up, and I'll shoot a hole through the middle and break it in two." She showed Caroline a small ear of colorful Indian corn. "Don't shake or move. If you do, you'll end up like the last Injun. Now get out."

As Caroline slid from the tent, she heard the rattle of glass and the distinctive slosh of whiskey. Sure Shot Sue was having a little nip.

10

Caroline was thankful that Sure Shot Sue's act came very early in the program, right after the grand entry. At least she did not have to go through the anguish of waiting for the dreaded moment.

Using a megaphone, the barker announced Sure Shot Sue in a howling loud voice, and the band played a drumroll as Sue ran and skipped into the arena, shooting her pistols into the air. They were blanks, Caroline had been told; but even so, women screamed and men cheered. This continued for about a minute before Sue reloaded her gun and settled into the routine.

Shawnee Sam operated an automatic spring-release machine that hurled colorful glass balls into the air. Sue shot them with accuracy, missing only one out of ten. Then she shot a few clay pigeons that didn't go as high. Next Sue did a few acrobatic tricks, shooting as she ran, shooting after rolling on the ground, shooting from the back of a lovely white horse that Caroline had been instructed to lead out into the arena.

Caroline's nerves began to relax a little as she watched Sue shoot a star pattern into a water barrel, making the water squirt out. Maybe the nip of whiskey was indeed helping steady Sue's hand.

At last it was time for Sue to shoot more dangerously, using real people. First she shot the ashes from a large cigar jutting from the lips of Shawnee Sam. Then she looked into a mirror and shot at the cigar again. This time his hat went flying. Sam grinned as if it were part of the act and replaced the cigar in his lips. Caroline noticed that he was trembling, but he did not even wince as the cigar exploded on the next shot.

Afterward, his fingers shook so that it was a miracle he could hold the ace of spades card before he tossed it in the air. Sue supposedly hit the center spade, but it was clear to Caroline that the hole was in the upper left corner.

Taking the megaphone away from the announcer, Shawnee Sam turned to Caroline and whispered, "What is your name?"

"Caroline," she replied in a trembling voice.

"I mean your Indian name," he insisted angrily. "Hurry."

Caroline's brain whirred as she looked at the packed stands and the hired hands and performers waiting in the sidelines. She glanced at the white horse and thought of her horse, Bellissimo. Suddenly she remembered the poster of her mother riding on a white horse.

"My name is Little Dancing Rain."

Sam crinkled up his brow, then put the horn to his lips.

"Here is a beautiful Indian princess, pure of heart and mind. She is the daughter of the great chief Standing Horse and granddaughter of the famous chief Looks-You-in-the-Eye. Ladies and gentlemen, I give to you Princess Little Dancing Rain."

The band imitated the sound of tom-tom drums.

The crowd applauded and cheered. After all, Caroline was the first Indian to perform that day. She didn't know what Shawnee Sam expected her to do, so she held up her hand in the greeting sign that she had seen all the Indians use when they met. Shawnee Sam showed Caroline where to stand and he put a small ear of red-and-yellow Indian corn in her hand, the smallest ear she had ever seen.

With a deep breath and a sense of doom, Caroline held it high in the air.

The crack of rifle fire and the explosion of the corn and the pain in Caroline's thumb occurred simultaneously. She looked down and saw a red gash across the top of her thumb and forefinger where Sue's bullet had grazed the flesh. Anger erupted inside Caroline as she shook her stinging hand.

The crowd went wild, thinking it was part of the act. Sam angrily handed Caroline another ear of corn.

"Put this between your teeth," he said.

Caroline swallowed hard, then crossed her arms and shook her head.

"I'd have to be insane to do that," Caroline whispered back at Sam. "Your wife is soused.

I'll wager that's not water in her drinking cup."

On seeing her stubborn refusal, the crowd roared with laughter. When Sam forced Caroline's hand open and slapped the ear of corn in it, she threw it at him. The crowd howled and hooted gleefully. Shawnee Sam's eyes turned into pits of green fire. If the crowd could have heard the words he uttered under his breath, they would have gasped for air.

"Put this in your hand, you little shrew, or you're out of the show."

"Better that than killed by your drunken wife's bullet. Her name should be Whiskey Shot Sue," Caroline hissed back. She tried to walk away, but Sam grabbed her arm and forced the corn back into her throbbing hand.

"Stand here and hold it again, or I'll thrash the daylights out of you."

"How dare you lay a hand on me? I'll have the police arrest you for molesting a lady." Caroline shot the words at his face, then broke free.

Shawnee Sam growled and came after her. Seeing no place to escape, Caroline quickly climbed onto the back of Sue's horse. Not to be outdone, Shawnee Sam leaped onto his stallion, and the chase around the arena commenced. The band broke into a lively tune, "Camptown Races," as if the running horses were a rehearsed part of the program.

The men in the audience cheered when Sam took out his lariat and hurled it at Caroline. The women cheered when Caroline ducked low until she was on the opposite side of the saddle and the rope landed harmlessly. As Caroline rode like a maniac, coming close to the stands, she heard women yelling at her.

"Go, girl! Show him what-for!"

Caroline felt the women encouraging her, and for a moment she felt that she was the symbol of every woman or girl who had been chastised or chased for no good cause by some bully of a brother or cousin or father or husband.

Someone at the far end of the arena must have felt sympathy for Caroline, because suddenly the gate opened. She urged the horse through it, just as Sam's next lasso crashed against the horse's rump.

Caroline's heart pounded and her knees shook so much she could hardly dismount the frothy horse. Crooked Feather ran to her and quickly wrapped a buffalo hide over her shoulders and head.

"Hide under this until I can get you away," he said as he steered her toward a secluded corner.

"Crooked Feather, hurry," a young red-headed man dressed in buckskin said as he passed by. "The attack on the pioneer cabin is starting in a few minutes." He adjusted the coonskin cap on his head and threw a long powder musket over his shoulder, then joined several other men and women and children all dressed in pioneer clothes. They fell in line behind a log cabin, mounted on a flat barge with wheels, being pulled by mules.

Crooked Feather nodded to his friend, then put his hands firmly on Caroline's shoulders.

"You were wonderful," he said, smiling. "You stood up to Sam like a true woman warrior."

"I assure you," Caroline said from beneath the buffalo hide, "it was a matter of survival, not courage, that made me do it."

In the arena the band played a sweet, steady tune while the pioneers pretended to chop wood, skin beavers, spin yarn on a spinning wheel, weave cloth on a loom, and bake bread. Suddenly the music changed to a menacing, faster beat, accentuated by a pounding tom-tom.

"There's the signal for the Indian attack on the settlers' cabin. I have to go now. Please stay hidden away from Shawnee Sam. You haven't seen his temper yet."

"No? Then what was that chase all about?"

"That was nothing compared to what he would do if he were truly mad. Believe my words, Princess Little Dancing Rain."

Caroline's face turned red and she slapped his bare arm. "Don't call me that ridiculous name."

"It is a good name. It fits you truly." Crooked Feather's dark eyes twinkled and Caroline knew he was enjoying teasing her—but he could not stay. He ran to catch up with the other Indians, who were mounting their painted ponies. A few minutes later the pounding of the drums increased and the yelps and whoops of the Indians and the thunder of their horses' hooves filled the arena as they circled around the settlers' cabin.

When Caroline smelled wood burning and

heard the crackle of fire, she sneaked to the edge of the canopy and watched the program. The act called for the burning of the cabin, but of course, they did not really burn it down. The Indians had merely shot burning arrows into bundles of hay placed around the cabin. When the Indians came back after the end of the act, their faces and horses were spotted with soot, so close did they come to the flames.

The Wild West show progressed, with one exciting event after another. Each group of performers waited its turn just outside the entry ropes, and the ramrod barked orders and lined them up.

The cowboys rode broncos and bulls; the Mexican vaqueros twirled ropes in the most exquisite manner, leaping in and out of the loops as agilely as cats. Distinguished guests from the audience rode in the stagecoach, including the mayor and city councilmen. As the brown-and-yellow coach rolled around the arena, suddenly a band of robbers swooped down upon it. The coach driver shouted and whipped the mules, and the race continued two times around the hippodrome.

The last part of the program, called

"Custer's Last Charge," was fast approaching, and the ramrod was pulling Indian women, old men, and children toward the rope. He shoved Caroline into line next to Afraid-of-Birds. On seeing the blue cotton stockings on the older woman, he tried to make her remove them, but Afraid-of-Birds loudly refused. After arguing and cursing, the ramrod finally gave up and Afraid-of-Birds grinned with pleasure as she strutted out to the arena, the only Indian with blue legs.

"Be thankful she decided not to wear the white petticoat today," Caroline whispered to the red-faced ramrod, then joined the other Indians shuffling to the far end of the hippo-drome, where a tepee had been set up. Afraid-of-Birds started a fire and the Indians began doing daily activities. The old men made bows and arrows and chipped flint to make arrow-heads. The children played games with sticks and stones. The women pretended to tan buf-falo hides and weave baskets.

A few moments later the music changed to become dark and moody, but the Indians con-tinued their chores.

With an explosion of loud music and the

charge of a cavalry bugle, a troop of mounted U.S. soldiers circled the camp. They shot blanks with their rifles and pistols. Two of the old Indian men clasped their chests and fell. The others picked up bows and arrows and fought back. The women and children scattered, screaming. Caroline did not have to pretend she was afraid, for the leader of the cavalry was none other than Shawnee Sam himself, and he recognized her.

The music grew sad as the cavalry rode off and all the Indian men, women, and children lay motionless on the field. Even the audience was silent for once.

Caroline heard voices and looked up to see Crooked Feather and a dozen other Indian braves riding in on painted horses. They saw the massacre, screamed for revenge, then decorated their faces with war paint and rode away to the far side of the arena.

The whooping and shouting and gun firing continued at the other end of the hippodrome when the Indians found the cavalry soldiers. While the stunned audience watched the cavalry being annihilated, the Indian women, children, and old men at the tepee got up and slipped out of the arena.

By the time Caroline looked back, the last of the cavalrymen, Shawnee Sam himself playing the role of Custer, stood with his sword bared, slashing at a bevy of Indians. The audience groaned and gasped as the Indians pretended to scalp the soldiers, then charged out of the arena.

The Indian braves laughed and joked as they dismounted their ponies behind the lines.

Caroline grabbed Crooked Feather's arm. "That act was awful. They killed all the poor soldiers."

"The poor soldiers? What about the poor Indians—women and children?"

Caroline thought a moment, then looked at the ground. "Oh. I suppose you are right. What are those men joking about?"

"Standing Horse says, 'One day I will scalp Shawnee Sam truly, and what a surprise he will have in his eyes!'"

Caroline shuddered. "Did you ever take a scalp?"

Crooked Feather sighed. "No. I was born on a reservation. I've never seen a battle, except here."

"You sound so disappointed."

"I am. I wish I had been born a hundred

years ago, before the buffalo were killed, before our lands were turned into farms. I would have been a great warrior then. I hate my life now."

"But why? The lives of the Indians are so much easier now. You don't have to worry about hunting food every day in the summer and starving in the winter. And always fighting other tribes."

Crooked Feather glared at Caroline.

"My grandfather told me that in the old days, when the reservations were new, the government gave us live cattle every month and we hunted them down with pride. It was like hunting buffalo, and a man could still show his worth. That was part of the agreement in the treaty my grandfathers signed. Later, the government tossed out slaughtered beef carcasses, often filled with worms and too rotten to eat. The suppliers kept the best meat and sold it illegally. They tossed out bags of mealy flour like you toss a bone to a dog. Later still the government destroyed the reservations and told the Indians to live in houses and farm like white men."

"I'm sorry. But at least your people are getting educated now. You could find work in the cities and not depend on the charity of the government."

Crooked Feather's dark eyes steamed with anger. "You speak like a white woman. I thought your heart was at least half Indian, but I guess I was wrong." He glanced up. "Here comes Shawnee Sam. Tell him your ideas, and he will know that you are not an Indian princess."

Caroline saw Sam bearing down on her like a locomotive at full steam. She started to run, but someone stepped in the way and she fell.

Sam lifted her up by one arm. "Princess Little Dancing Rain. That was a very interesting show you put on. Fortunately for you, the audience loved it. I've decided to leave it in. You'll do the same thing, only ride around the arena two times and do more tricks. The ducking down was good, but also go under the horse's neck and then come up on the opposite side. And pretend you almost fall off and climb back on. The crowd will love it."

He glanced at the gash on her thumb. "And I guess I'll tell Sue to use blanks in her gun for your act. Now go out there and autograph and let them take your picture. You get to keep half of what tips they give you." He pushed Caroline toward the back lot, where hundreds of people were milling about.

Caroline stood next to the old chiefs with the feather warbonnets that gracefully flowed to the ground. Spectators paid a dime for a souvenir photograph and paid the Indians a dime to autograph it. Caroline felt foolish standing there, but to her surprise, several children and women came up to her and asked her to autograph the program.

"The princess doesn't know how to write," Shawnee Sam lied. "But she'll be happy to put her mark on your paper for a dime."

Illiterate, indeed! Caroline started to protest, but Sam gave her his evil eye. She drew some gibberish on the paper with a flourish and heard the women *ooh* in delight.

"You very brave," one of the women said, waving her hands to accentuate her words.

Caroline wanted to say, *"You very stupid to pay a dime for my autograph,"* but she restrained herself. Besides, her meager funds had been exhausted, and the money would come in handy. To her amazement, soon a line had formed, nearly all women and girls. Some shook her hand and examined the genuine cut made by Sure Shot Sue's bullet.

Caroline noticed that Billy Big Tree was not signing, nor was he posing for the photographer. His wrinkled face remained stern and emotionless as white people walked around him, touching his feathers and moccasins. A few offered him money, but he refused.

Caroline's heart broke in two when she saw some boys poking a stick at him. She could not bear it another moment and stomped to his side.

"Leave him alone," she said, grabbing the stick from one boy's hand. "He's not an old dog to be prodded and poked at. He's a human being."

"He's just an old Injun."

"Ha!" Caroline put her hands on her hips and leaned down close to the boy's face. "He's Chief Billy Big Tree. Why, he has scalped more men and women and little annoying children like you than there are freckles on your nose. Just the other day he was telling me that his fingers were getting stiff from lack of use, and I had to get on my knees and beg him not to go out and scalp somebody for the exercise."

The freckle-faced boy swallowed hard. His friends clutched each other and stepped back.

"Now, you apologize to Mr. Big Tree, and maybe he'll not slip into your house tonight while you're asleep and skin you alive."

"I—I'm sorry," the boy said, his voice trembling and his eyes moist with tears.

"We're sorry," the others said, then they turned tail and ran.

Caroline sighed in satisfaction, then glanced at Billy Big Tree. She doubted that he could speak any English, so he probably did not know what had just transpired. His face remained emotionless as he puffed on a very old, worn pipe. His clothes were more raggedy than the other chiefs' and it was downright embarrassing how much dirt clung to them.

"I'd be happy to patch your pants and your shirt, sir," Caroline offered.

Silence.

"I've collected a bit of money today from the spectators, and I'd be able to purchase some thread and needle and whatever it takes. Those beads on your sleeve are coming loose."

Silence.

"Why won't you speak to me? Don't you understand English?" Caroline glanced around hoping to see Crooked Feather, but he was no-where in sight.

She dropped to her knees, making her face lower than Big Tree's. She pointed to the elaborate beadwork fastened around her neck.

"This belonged to my mother, Princess Dancing Rain. I think you knew her. I don't want to cause any trouble, sir. I just want to find out where she came from and who her relatives are. I won't interfere, but I have to know. It's like a burning fire in my belly that won't get doused out with anything but the pure truth."

The old man's eyes remained fixed on the distant horizon, unflinching and calm.

"All right, Mr. Big Tree, you win this match. But the next time I talk to you I will have someone to translate, and there will be no excuse for your silence. I promise you, if you know about my mother, I will find out."

Thus ended Caroline Elizabeth Long's first conversation with Billy Big Tree. One-sided though it was, she felt that it was the beginning of a great change about to come into her life.

The truth was somewhere inside the wrinkled brown face and sad eyes. Whether that knowledge would destroy her world or bring her peace, Caroline could not say. But one thing she knew for sure: Nothing would stop her from finding out the truth.

11

After all the spectators had cleared the lots and the roustabouts had filled the saloons and gambling houses, Caroline thought she would spend a restful evening doing nothing. But as soon as she arrived at the tepee, Afraid-of-Birds put her to work. First she helped to gather twigs and dry grass to start a fire, then she was taught the fine art of skinning a rabbit that had had the misfortune of stumbling into the Indian campgrounds. Afraid-of-Birds, her sister, and the children found Caroline to be an unequaled source of entertainment and giggled the whole evening at everything she did.

From across the camp the smell of soup from the metal barrels enticed Caroline; but she was too tired to walk even that short distance, so she ate rabbit and hominy. Afterward, she curled up on a buffalo hide and fell into an exhausted sleep.

The next morning, Crooked Feather rounded up a horse for Caroline, since Sure Shot Sue was not very happy that Caroline had used hers in the show.

The horse was a beautiful pinto, with a sweet face and intelligent eyes. Caroline named her Belle.

"This horse belonged to Standing Horse's daughter," Crooked Feather explained as he placed the lightweight Indian saddle on the horse's back. "She was training it to do tricks."

"What kind of tricks?"

"Shawnee Sam wanted this horse to perform like Sitting Bull's famous horse that sat on its haunches and pawed the air. And he wanted it to rear up like a fighting stallion."

Caroline stroked the brown-and-white-splotched neck. "Did Belle learn those things?"

"No. But she is very smart and will let you move around on her back without becoming frightened or breaking her stride. But even so, it is important that you do not make sudden movements, or she will become confused about what you want her to do."

Caroline felt exhilarated to be on a horse again, even though the saddle was not as heavy and sturdy as the one she was used to and she was forced to straddle the horse like a man. When Caroline had ridden Bellissimo, Grandmother Long and Aunt Oriona had always insisted she ride sidesaddle, like a lady. Sometimes, when they weren't watching, Caroline had used a man's saddle and straddled the horse. She enjoyed the freedom of riding like that, but her petticoats had bunched up and gotten in the way. Now, dressed in buckskin leggings, she felt comfortable and natural.

It took a while for Caroline to get used to mounting from the right, the way the Indians did, but soon she was concentrating on learning to slide from one side of the horse to the other, first as the horse walked, then as it trotted. Belle performed beautifully, seemingly not bothered by the weight on her back shifting from one side to the other. Crooked Feather stood by, his bare chest covered with perspiration as he helped Caroline in and out of the saddle repeatedly.

Around midmorning Shawnee Sam, who

was riding by on his magnificent Appaloosa, took a few minutes to watch Caroline.

"You're very talented," he said, nodding his approval. "I'm going to tell one of the Cossack riders to teach you a couple of tricks. If your act proves popular, I'll increase your pay by a dollar a week."

Caroline's mouth flew open. "Thank you, sir," she said.

After a long pause in which Shawnee Sam peered into Caroline's face, he clucked to his horse and rode away.

Crooked Feather let out a long breath.

"That was a close call," he whispered. "I think Shawnee Sam is getting suspicious."

"Suspicious of what? That I am the daughter of Dancing Rain? Maybe he remembers her. Maybe I should speak to him about it."

"No, I meant suspicious that you are not on the official list of Indian performers. That you are an illegal stowaway."

"What will Sam do if he finds out?"

"He will be very upset. He could get into big trouble for taking an Indian out of Indian Territory without the government's permission. He signed a contract with the Indian

Agency to provide our food and supplies and pay us a monthly salary. And he had to put up a five thousand dollar bond to insure that he would bring us all back safely."

"But I'm not an Indian!" Caroline insisted.

Crooked Feather glanced at her. Two days in the bright sun had already turned her olive complexion a shade darker than it had ever been.

"I'm afraid Shawnee Sam won't believe that. If he catches you, he'll probably send you back."

"Back to a reservation?"

"Not exactly a reservation."

"But I thought all Indians lived on reservations. Put there for your own good—that's what my schoolteacher said."

"Did she also tell you about the Dawes Act?"

Caroline shook her head slowly, almost afraid to hear what she knew he would surely say.

Crooked Feather smiled lightly, as if tolerating an ignorant child.

"Once my ancestors lived free as the wind, going where they pleased, following the great buffalo herds. Then they signed treaties and agreed to live on large portions of land called reservations. Each tribe was granted its own area, to live on as it pleased. The reserved areas were smaller than the Great Plains, but at least the land was theirs. They still lived in tepees and had their own tribal governments, the way it had been for generations. Since there were no more buffalo, they were to receive cows and flour and a constant supply of food."

"That doesn't sound too bad."

"No, but the government in Washington was not satisfied with that arrangement. The Dawes Act was passed to destroy our tribal ways and take the lands from us. All the Indian lands were divided so that each man received a small allotment of one hundred sixty acres for his whole family to live on. The leftover communal lands—millions of acres—were sold to white settlers."

"I've heard about the Cherokee Land Rush. I think my father was there, but he sold the piece of land he staked." Caroline almost felt ashamed to say it, but Crooked Feather did not seem to be angry at her.

"We were expected to live in houses like the

White Man," he continued. "And to become farmers and raise cows. My people were never farmers. We were warriors and disdained farmers like the Wichita and Cherokee. My ancestors raided enemy corn houses every fall. After the Dawes Act, some of my people died because they did not want to farm, or because they farmed poorly." Crooked Feather paused. "It is a bad time to be Indian."

"Is that why so many Indians want to travel with Shawnee Sam's Wild West show?"

Crooked Feather nodded. "At least in the show they can still pretend to hunt and to battle and to kill white men." He glanced at Caroline's startled face.

"Don't worry, Caroline, your scalp is safe with me. Far better you worry about Shawnee Sam and the government in Washington."

"That's outrageous. This is America. No one would treat *me* like that." She put her hands on her hips.

"You'd be surprised what can happen if people think you're an Indian."

"Don't be silly. You've got the same rights as I do," Caroline insisted, tossing her long braids over her shoulder.

Crooked Feather laughed lightly. "Do you truly believe that, Princess Little Dancing Rain?"

"Yes, of course."

Crooked Feather remained silent as they walked to the chuck wagon. Caroline had decided that stew and corn bread were more appealing than Afraid-of-Birds's rabbit and fry bread in the tepee.

While waiting in line, Caroline noticed the rude roustabout with the bushy black beard who had teased her two days before. He stared at her and Crooked Feather with small colorless eyes, then jabbed his friend in the ribs.

"Ugh! Injun heap big hungry. Eat-um all up," he said in an artificially deep voice.

Laughter rippled down the line.

Caroline glanced at Crooked Feather, who remained silent, staring ahead as if he did not hear the cruel words or laughter. They moved forward in the line slowly.

A moment later the roustabout spoke again. "It not buffalo meat, but by God, it no cost me nothing."

Laughter rippled again. Caroline saw

Crooked Feather's gaze drop to his feet and saw the pulse on his neck jump faster.

Caroline held out her metal bowl as the cook emptied a ladle of hot stew into it, then slapped a chunk of thick corn bread on top of that. Ashes from his cigar fell into the bowl, but he shoved it back at her without an apology.

"Ugh! Soup make-um big and strong," the roustabout teased as he rubbed his hands together and grinned. As Caroline and Crooked Feather walked past the line to leave, the man placed his fingers behind his head like feathers, did a little dance, and made whooping noises.

Caroline stopped and turned. Without a word, she dumped her bowl of hot stew on the man's feet.

"Ugh," she said. "Me so stupid, me stumble."

Crooked Feather tossed his bowl at the man, grabbed Caroline's hand, and they ran like the wind. They dodged through the tents, hid behind the grandstands, then worked their way back to the tepee.

As Caroline sat near the fire chewing a piece of fry bread, she glanced at Crooked Feather eating with a hearty appetite.

"All right," Caroline said at last. "You were right."

As he climbed to his feet, he nodded. "Unfortunately so."

Early the next morning a Cossack named Boris demonstrated how to ride with one foot in the stirrup, how to flip-flop from one side of the horse to the other, how to bounce off the ground and land back in the saddle, and how to ride under a horse's belly.

Good heavens! Caroline thought as she watched the agile man in the baggy Turkish pants, short jacket, and tremendously long mustache. *It will take me years to master those tricks.* However, with diligent practice all morning, she was able to learn to shift from one side of the horse to the other and knew that it was only a matter of time until she would learn to slip under the horse's belly. After landing on her bottom several times, she decided that doing vaults was not one of her born talents.

Caroline's little pinto was wonderfully patient and intelligent. She allowed Caroline to rove over her back like a spider and even learned to rear on demand.

In that afternoon's show, Caroline's act was as popular as before, and she got more applause than Shawnee Sam when she dodged his lariat.

Caroline's part in the show drew more attention, and after the third day, Shawnee Sam hired a photographer to take Caroline's picture sitting on top of her horse and to make prints to sell to the public.

"You're learning very fast," Shawnee Sam said after the photographer left. "I'm surprised that I didn't notice you before now. You say you're with your grandfather? Who might that be?"

She glanced around for Crooked Feather, but he was across the camp practicing with his bow and arrows.

"Wa-tah-ki-gosh-tah-ki-so." Caroline said a mouthful of made-up gibberish.

"Hmm, I don't recall that name."

Caroline shrugged and started to leave, but Shawnee Sam took her elbow. His intense green eyes examined her face, as he had done every time he saw her.

"Tell me, why are you called Princess Little Dancing Rain?"

Caroline felt her pulse quicken and her ears grow hot.

"I like the rain. I like to dance in the rain."

"I see. And the word *Little*?"

"I've been doing it since I was a child. A *little* child."

"Hmm." He stroked his blond goatee. "Well, I suppose it's just a coincidence, but I used to have a young Indian performer named Princess Dancing Rain."

Caroline caught her breath.

"As a matter of fact, you remind me of her. She, too, loved horses and rode more like a warrior than a girl. She was so agile. And what balance! She could do a handstand on her horse's back, turn directions, and then sit backward. She could grab the tail of a running horse and manage to climb up into the saddle from the rear. Now, very few men, even, can do that. I must say she was one of the best acts we had. And very well liked by the audience and the other performers. She had a way about her, very naive and worldly at the same time. She trusted everyone."

Caroline realized she had been holding her breath and exhaled slowly.

"What happened to her?" she asked in hardly more than a whisper.

Shawnee Sam glanced at Caroline, then busied himself putting on his fringed buckskin gloves.

"I'm not sure. She vanished one day while we were performing in Chicago. I had a devil of a time explaining to the Indian Agency what had happened. We finally put her down as an accidental drowning victim, since she was fond of riding along the river wherever we traveled. Her horse vanished, too."

"Didn't any of her people know what happened?"

Shawnee Sam snorted. "Of course I interrogated all the Indians and even tried to bribe Billy Big Tree, but his lips were sealed. I took it to be a tribal taboo to speak of the dead."

Caroline's eyes grew larger and she twisted the reins in her hands. Her mouth had gone dry and she found it difficult to speak. But at last she forced the words out.

"Why was it that you interrogated Billy Big Tree? Was he a relative?"

Shawnee Sam swung up onto his horse.

"Yes, indeed. Billy was Dancing Rain's father."

Rage boiled in Caroline's heart as she stomped across the campground to the tepee where Billy Big Tree lived. He was sitting outside of it, his knees crossed and, as always, a pipe between his lips.

Without a word of greeting, Caroline stood in front of him, her hands on her hips.

"You know who I am," she insisted. "And I know who you are, *Grandfather*."

For the first time the old man looked up. His eyes, dim with age, studied Caroline's face, then he returned to his pipe without speaking.

Caroline expelled air in a hiss.

"Don't you want to know what happened to your daughter, Dancing Rain? Don't you want to know if she is alive, or dead, or happily married—or what her fate has been all these years?"

The old man still did not speak, but he stopped smoking the pipe. It rested loosely in his withered hands, the thin gray smoke curling up around his weathered face.

Caroline sighed. "I know you are my grandfather, and denying it won't make me go away. Now that my father's run off again and my aunt hates me, you're all I've got left." Caroline dropped to her knees and tried to take one of the old hands in her own, but it was stiff and uncooperative.

"I think you understand me, but you just don't want to have anything to do with me because I'm half-white. Well, maybe I don't want to have anything to do with you either, old man." Caroline felt tears blurring his image. "I just thought you might like to know when and how Dancing Rain died, but I guess I was wrong. You don't care about anybody or anything except for that pipe. Well, you've made it plain that you don't want to have anything to do with me, so I won't be bothering you anymore."

Caroline rose to her feet and ran. Even when she heard Big Tree's crackled voice begin to sing a high-pitched song and heard the tap of his small drum, she did not stop.

As she approached the tepee of Standing Horse, she brushed past Crooked Feather. He caught her by the sleeve.

"What happened? What did you say to Big Tree a moment ago?"

"Nothing that matters."

"You must have said something very important. He is singing the death song of his people."

"What do you mean?"

"It is the song an Indian sings when he learns of the death of a loved one."

Caroline swirled around and looked at Big Tree, his callused brown hands tapping out a steady beat on the drum and his voice raised to a sad, stirring pitch.

"He is mourning the death of his daughter," she said softly.

12

At the end of the first week, after the last show of the day, Caroline saw Crooked Feather walking toward her, carrying a buckskin pouch. Without saying a word, he dropped it into her hand.

"What is this? A medicine bag?" she asked as her fingers touched the soft, pliable deerskin decorated with beads.

"No. It's for all that money you've been saving."

A grin spread across Caroline's face. "Thank you, Crooked Feather. Can you believe I've saved ten dollars just from signing photographs and posing with customers?"

"Surely I can. Your act is one of the most

popular with the women and girls. I think they admire you for standing up to Shawnee Sam."

"Well, whatever the reason, I'm collecting tips at an amazing pace. And at the end of the month I'll collect wages, too, just like you."

She glanced at the deerskin medicine bag that Crooked Feather wore around his neck. Caroline knew it was filled with secret healing herbs and sacred stones and mementos of his life that had meaning only to him. She wondered if he kept his money there, too.

"Do you have a lot of money saved up, Crooked Feather? You told me once that this is your second season with Shawnee Sam."

"True, it is, but I do not have much money. It slips through my fingers like water, and I don't know where it goes... All the performers have the afternoon off. Some of them are going into town to see the sights. Would you like to go with me?"

"That sounds entertaining. Should I change back into my cotton skirt and blouse?"

"I don't think Afraid-of-Birds can be persuaded to part with your petticoat and stockings. I saw her down by the river washing clothes, and her legs were blue."

"Then I will wear what I have on. Maybe

the townspeople will enjoy seeing a couple of Indians walking down the street. I'll run and fetch my money. Meet me in front of the ticket booth."

Caroline hustled back to the tepee. She combed and rebraided her hair, washed her face, and straightened her buckskin leggings. She scooped her nickels, dimes, and pennies into the new leather pouch, then tied it around her neck. The money felt heavy and jingled as she trotted across the field to the ticket booth.

To her amazement, Crooked Feather had changed into a calico shirt, string tie, stiff dark denim pants, suspenders, and cowboy boots and hat. She could not help but burst into laughter.

"What are you doing dressed like that?"

"These are the kinds of clothes I wore after I graduated from boarding school."

"Now I know why you have no money," Caroline said as she grabbed his hand and ran after a buckboard wagon loaded with performers on their way to town.

When the wagon reached the main street, the passengers flowed out like a spilled bucket of squealing rats and swooped down onto the unsuspecting shops.

Caroline could have spent her money freely

on anything she wanted, but as they strolled the streets, gazing into windows, she saw nothing that appealed to her. Dolls seemed so childish now, and fancy clothes and knickknacks were pointless.

As they stepped from the bright sunlight into a general merchandise store, the smell of food and dry goods filled Caroline's head with memories of trips to town with her grandmother. Crooked Feather made a beeline for three huge wooden barrels near the counter. He lifted the first lid, saw salted pork, and slammed it shut. He lifted the second lid, saw crackers, and closed it back. When he lifted the third lid, he smiled and reached inside.

"This is what I like," he said, holding a monstrous pickle in his fingers. He slid a nickel onto the counter and bit into the sour cylinder with glee.

"Mmm. Delicious. Try it." He offered the pickle to Caroline.

Caroline took a small bite, made a face, then declined his next offer. The smell and taste of the pickle sent memories hurling into her head. Many times she had helped Ester gather cucumbers from the garden behind the house and watched her pickle them in a sour mixture of vinegar, salt, and water. One day Taffy and Caroline sneaked into the root cellar and ate a whole jar. That night their teeth ached so much they couldn't even stand to drink water.

Caroline sighed. She had wanted to come to town, but now everything she saw only reminded her of her home and her grandmother—bags of dried beans slumped on the floor; bins of flour, cornmeal, and sugar; coffee beans; tins of store tea; bolts of calico and gingham cloth; kitchen utensils, butter churns, jars of elixirs claiming to cure every ailment.

By the time Caroline had circled back to the cashier's counter, she saw Crooked Feather stooped over the jars of candy, putting down his nickels and pennies for an assortment of peanut brittle, taffy, fudge, licorice, and gumdrops, and a fistful of hard candy sticks.

She watched in amazement as he strolled to the dry goods section and purchased colored ribbons, a patch of red velvet, and three cat's-eye marbles. After handing over the last of his money, he turned around, his arms full.

"See what I mean?" He shrugged. "Money flies from my fingers like a frightened sparrow. Aren't you going to buy anything?"

"There is nothing here I want for myself,

but perhaps..." She walked back to the counter where the tobacco products were displayed— cigars; chewing tobacco pressed into hard, dark rectangles; small boxes of snuff; packs of thin papers for rolling cigarettes; pipes; and tins filled with various grades of shredded tobacco.

"How much for this?" she asked the clerk, pointing to a tin of tobacco with the picture of an Indian chief on the front.

"One dollar and six bits."

As Caroline counted out the money, Crooked Feather crinkled up his thick eyebrows. "Who is that for?"

"It's for Billy Big Tree. Do you think he will like this brand?"

"The brand doesn't matter. Big Tree always mellows his tobacco out with sumac and tree bark," Crooked Feather said.

"That's what you Injuns call *kinnikinnic*," the store clerk said as he handed Caroline her change. "You ought to know that, little gal."

Caroline felt her face turning red. She grabbed the tobacco and hurried out the door.

In an alley beside the store, a noisy group of boys was playing a game of mumblety-peg. Crooked Feather put his goods on the ground and walked up to the boy holding the jack-knife.

"May I?" he asked, and took the knife from the boy's trembling hand.

Crooked Feather aimed the knife at a circle in the dirt. It neatly flipped over in the air several times before its blade stuck in the firm ground.

The boys screamed, stumbled over each other, and ran down the alley in terror.

"Wait! Come back! I just wanted to play one game..." Crooked Feather's voice trailed to a whisper. "I was the undefeated champion in boarding school." He stared at the vanishing boys, his lips turned down in a frown, then he grabbed his parcels. "I should have known that would happen. It always does when I try to play with white boys. They are afraid of me. Me, who never even killed a buffalo or deer or measly rabbit, much less a man or boy."

"Boys are silly, anyway," Caroline said.

"But why are they afraid of me? I'm wearing White Man's clothes. I eat White Man's food." He lifted up a pickle and a bag of penny candy. "I buy White Man's trinkets." Suddenly he dropped the bags to the ground and kicked them. The marbles rolled down the alley and the hard candy broke into pieces.

"Crooked Feather! What are you doing?"

"These are White Man's things." He ripped the string tie from around his neck. "I should be buying glass beads and buckskin and tobacco. I should be wearing buffalo skins and deer antlers like my uncles. They would never be caught in a dry goods store buying penny candy. I feel so ashamed."

Crooked Feather dashed his string tie to the ground and ran down the street, pushing by a troupe of show performers who were carrying bottles of whiskey and singing bawdy tunes.

Caroline salvaged all the items she could and left the rest to a stray dog that wagged its tail and licked the broken candy. She caught a ride back to the fairgrounds in a carriage with Shawnee Sam and Sure Shot Sue, who had spent the afternoon at a keno parlor where Sam had won twenty-five dollars.

As usual, Sue smelled of liquor. While the carriage gently rocked, she fell into a deep, snore-filled sleep.

"I suppose you've spent all your money," Sam said to Caroline, winking. "All the youngsters and Indians do. I'll bet you spent your first dime on one of those sideshows that hang around my extravaganza."

Caroline had seen the creepy sideshows camped on the outer fringes of the Wild West tents, where barkers shouted out the gross details of human deformities—twins joined at the hip, a tiny man only three feet tall, a grotesquely large woman with a beard as thick as any man's. Of all the sideshows, the only one that interested Caroline was the contortionist's—a man so limber he was said to be able to tie his body in a knot.

"No, sir. I've bought some tobacco for my grandfather. I'm saving the rest of my money for something special."

"Ooh-la-la." Sam rolled his eyes and tugged at his blond goatee. "Maybe a wedding trousseau? I think Crooked Feather would like to make you his bride, Little Dancing Rain. If that happens, I could have the ceremony during one of the shows. I can see it now." He lifted his hands as if peering through a viewing glass, and his green eyes stared into space as he imagined the scene. "By Jove, what a crowd pleaser it would be. And Heaven knows I need something to attract more people. These folks are holding on to their money like a bunch of pikers."

Caroline felt heat rising up her cheeks and neck. How dare the old fool think of making a show out of something as personal and special as a girl's wedding? She had to count to ten before she had composed herself.

"I believe you are mistaken, sir. Crooked Feather has no such feelings for me. Why, I am not even an Indian—"

"What!"

Caroline caught her breath. "An Indian from the same tribe, sir, I meant to say."

"Oh, I see. Well, Crooked Feather is not like the others. He's more civilized and wouldn't hold that against you."

"But, sir, I'm not fourteen yet, though my birthday is fast approaching. I'm too young to marry anyone."

"Balderdash! I've seen you Indian girls become squaws at thirteen. Think it over. I'll pay you a handsome bonus to have your wedding ceremony in the arena."

A loud snore and a snort from Sure Shot Sue broke the silence, and Caroline was more than happy to feel the carriage slow and see the show tents come into view. Another moment with Shawnee Sam and he would be wanting to promote the birth of her first child.

As Caroline walked to the tepees, she felt the still-heavy bag of coins jingling against her chest. She had not mentioned to anyone why she was saving her money, for she had not been sure herself until she arrived back at the tepee and saw Afraid-of-Birds sewing a patch on Standing Horse's tunic.

Suddenly Caroline knew exactly what she would do with her money. Through sign language, the few words of Kiowa that she had learned, and the few words of English the older woman had learned, Caroline asked Afraid-of-Birds how difficult it would be to make a new chief's ensemble for Billy Big Tree, with fine beads and quillwork for decoration. Afraid-of-Birds said it would take her at least two moons to make it and the materials would be expensive.

"Me not Wichita," the older woman confessed in choppy English. "Wichita woman must do work."

Caroline removed her mother's beaded neckband.

"This is a Wichita pattern. Can you use it?"

Afraid-of-Birds shook her head.

"Pattern sacred. I no do."

Caroline was befuddled and mad all at the same time.

"All those silly rules. This belonged to my mother. Can't I copy this pattern?"

Afraid-of-Birds nodded. "You do it, not me. I teach you quill and bead."

Caroline was so excited about the prospect of making her grandfather some new clothes that she'd almost forgotten about the tin of tobacco. She hurried to the old man's tent. He sat in front of it, in the same position he had sat in every day that Caroline visited him the past week, legs crossed, the pipe in his mouth.

"Grandfather," she said softly, and tiptoed closer.

The old man puffed on his pipe, his dark eyes shadowed by craggy white eyebrows. As usual, he gave no indication that he'd noticed her.

"I brought you a gift. It's tobacco for your pipe." She placed the colorful tin in front of him, then knelt across from him. "It's a good brand."

Big Tree continued puffing, and Caroline once again wondered why she was wasting her time trying to soften his stony heart.

"You can mellow it with sumac and tree bark to make *kinnikinnic*." She repeated what she had learned from Crooked Feather earlier that day.

"Hmmph!" Big Tree grunted.

Caroline nearly jumped out of her skin, and her mouth opened as she watched him take the pipe out of his mouth.

"Where did you learn of *kinnikinnic*?" he said in slow, deliberate English.

"Crooked Feather told me it was an Indian custom," she said, trying not to show her utter amazement.

"That Lost Child knows nothing about being an Indian."

"He knows more than I do."

Caroline thought she saw a tiny smile flicker on the wrinkled old lips, but she dared not hope for so good a sign. Moments passed before Big Tree finished his pipe. He slowly opened the new tin, pinched some tobacco between his fingers, and sniffed it. He nodded, then reclosed the lid.

Caroline sat in silence, wondering if she

should say something more but knowing that anything she said could be cause for his withdrawal.

At last Big Tree rose to his feet and went inside the tepee..Caroline's heart sank and she lowered her head, fighting back the tears. She had tried for days to befriend the old man and had even offered to help him with his chores, but he always turned his back on her and vanished inside the tepee, like now.

As Caroline rose to leave, the flaps of the tepee moved and Big Tree reemerged, holding something small and shiny. He extended his hand and Caroline saw a gold locket twinkling in the sunlight.

She sucked in her breath. "For me?" she gasped.

"You give me gift. I give you gift. It is all I have of value."

"Oh, but you don't have to give me anything. You are my grandfather. I gave the tobacco to you freely..." She paused, seeing his expression of annoyance. She took the locket, feeling its smooth, cool surface. "Thank you."

Caroline pried open the clasp with her fingernail, wondering where it had come from, praying that it was not stained with the blood of some unfortunate pioneer girl. Expecting to find the portrait of a strange blond or red-headed person, Caroline gasped in shock when she saw the tiny image of a beautiful dark-haired, dark-eyed Indian woman.

"It's, it's...oh, my! It's my mother, isn't it?"

Big Tree nodded. "She bought it in Chicago and gave it to me before she ran away."

Caroline's heart soared with joy and before she knew what she was doing, she threw her arms around the old man and sobbed onto his narrow, bony shoulder.

"Oh, thank you, Grandfather. Thank you. I shall cherish this forever."

The old man did not return her hug, but Caroline thought she felt the faintest touch of his hand on her hair. Perhaps she was wrong, but she decided to accept her heart's imagining. She slid the locket around her neck and kissed the picture before snapping it closed. "Can you tell me about my mother? I want to learn everything about her."

"Sit down, child," Big Tree said, waving at

the blanket in front of the tepee. Caroline helped him lower his body, then sat across from him.

"There are more things about our people that you do not know than blades of grass on the prairie. They could take a lifetime to learn."

Caroline patted the blanket. "Well, I'm not going anywhere very soon. And you've got to start sometime. Didn't that old Chinese man say that a journey of a thousand miles begins with a single step?"

Big Tree squinted at her, then nodded.

"He was a wise man. So let your journey begin this day." He dug into the new tin of tobacco and withdrew a pinch of the dark brown shreds. Then he opened the pouch around his neck, removed some dried leaves, and mixed them with the tobacco; then stuffed it all into his pipe and lit it. He drew several puffs.

"The first thing you must learn is that among our people, the names of the dead are never mentioned."

"Why is that?" Caroline asked.

"I will answer your question with a story," Big Tree said, and began in a steady, even voice: "Once a brave young warrior lost his beautiful wife. He loved her more than the deer in the forest, more than the eagles in the sky. The young man's friends prepared her for burial, bathing her corpse, dressing her in her finest clothes, and painting her face with sacred symbols. When all the relatives had gathered from neighboring villages, they dug a shallow grave on the side of a hill.

"The shaman said a sacred prayer to Earth Mother: 'Earth Mother, you contain all things, you produce all things, and you allow us to travel on your back. We have been told to take care of everything from your bosom, and we have been told that every living thing should be returned to your soil. We come to bury this woman.'

"Then they lowered her body and turned her head to face east. They put her favorite possessions inside—a basket, a clay pot, and a beaded neckband. They covered her body and encircled the grave with logs. For four days the young man and the girl's relatives mourned her, dressing in rags and neither washing nor combing their hair. Four times a day they bathed in a stream for purification.

"On the fourth day, the final rites of

mourning commenced. The mourners sat in robes and passed a pipe among themselves. They wept and friends wiped their tears and washed their faces. The village leader announced that the mourning period was over, and a feast was held.

"The husband of the girl cut his long braids, washed his body, and received new clothing. All his wife's possessions were given away and new ones furnished by friends. It was time to move on with his life, but the young husband could not forget his beautiful wife. His heart was heavy with sorrow and nothing his friends or relatives said could make him happy again.

"Now, this young man knew that it was forbidden ever to mention the names of the dead again, but he did not understand why. During the day, among the villagers, he obeyed this promise. But one night, while Bright Shining Woman stood in the night sky and shed her golden light on the sleeping village, the husband sneaked to the place where his wife had been buried. There he fell to his knees, and with tears falling from his eyes, he called out her name again and again.

"Suddenly the earth shook and he heard a great pitiful moan. A pale image of his wife appeared above the grave. So filled with fright was the man that he could not move. Her skin was decayed and her eye sockets hollow.

" 'Here I am, beloved,' she said. 'I heard you speak my name all the way from the spirit world. I miss you so much I must have you with me.' And with those words, she seized his hands and pulled him down into the grave with her. The next day the villagers found his moccasins and his medicine bag on the ground, but he was never seen again."

Big Tree puffed his pipe, sending little round clouds of smoke into the cool evening air.

Caroline swallowed hard.

"Is that true?"

"If you want it to be true, it is."

"That story scared me. But I don't think it really happened. I've heard Aunt Oriona mention the names of dead people before. She loves to talk about dead people."

"Then you have nothing to fear by mentioning the names of the dead. As for me, I will not do it."

"Then how will I learn about my mother?"

"I will tell you stories about the village. You will learn about her people, and knowing them, you will know her." Big Tree glanced at the setting sun. "Man-Reflecting-Light is going to bed. And so must I." He tapped the spent tobacco ashes from the pipe and tucked it away in the bag around his neck, then struggled to rise to his feet.

Caroline jumped up and took his elbow. His body felt light as a stick, but it was still strong. She rolled up his blanket and placed it inside the tepee beside his buffalo-hide bed.

"It's very unkempt in here," Caroline said, glancing around. "Look at those old corncobs, and the pile of rags and the broken baskets. It looks like you are in mourning for someone."

She turned to see Big Tree staring at her with a startled expression on his face.

"I'll come by tomorrow morning and clean it for you, if you like," she continued. "You can tell me another story. Is that all right with you?"

"I will tell you more stories. I will tell you about Kinnikasus, who created Morning Star, the First Man, and Bright Shining Woman, the moon. I will tell you about the South Star and

244

the North Star and all those beings we worship. And after I have told you many stories and you understand your mother's people, you will have to choose which path you will take—the Indian path or the White Man's path."

"Do I have to choose? Can't I belong to both worlds?"

Big Tree shook his head slowly, making his silvery hair tremble.

"If you try to take both paths, you will become a Lost Child."

"Like Crooked Feather?"

"Yes."

"Why does everyone call him that? He truly wants to be accepted by his people, but they won't let him be. Why?"

"It is not they who do not accept him. It is he who has not accepted them. One day he says, 'I am Indian,' and he does Indian things. But another day he says, 'Indian ways are bad. I will not do them anymore.' He lives with one foot in the White Man's world and the other in the Indian world. Until he sets both feet solidly in one place, he will not be able to stand."

"Do you think he will ever become Indian again?"

"Crooked Feather is like a man lost in the

woods. It is easy to stray off the path in bright daylight in search of sweet honey and tempting berries. But finding the path again in the dark is hard to do. Many die in the woods."

"Just like that song about the babes in the woods. Grandmother used to sing it to me at night while I was in bed." Caroline cleared her throat and sang in a sweet, clear voice:

Oh, dear, don't you know, how a long time ago
Two little babes, whose names I don't know
Went strolling away on a bright summer day
And were lost in the woods, I've heard people say.

And when it was night, so sad was their plight,
The moon had gone down, the stars gave no light;
They sobbed and they sighed, and oh how they cried,
Then the poor little babes lay down and they died.

Caroline stopped singing. "Do you know that song, Grandfather?"

"No, but it is a good story. What happened to the children?"

Caroline helped the old man stretch out on the buffalo hide. She poured cool water on a cloth and washed his face, then gave him a cup of fresh water to drink. As he closed his eyes, she sang the final verse of the song:

And when they were dead, the robins so red
Brought strawberry leaves and over them spread,
And sang them a song the whole summer long,
Poor babes in the woods, who never did wrong.

When she heard the old man breathing slowly, she leaned over and kissed his wrinkled cheek.

"I do not want to be a Lost Child, Grandfather," she whispered, then stole out of his tepee. The full moon shone through the tree branches and glistened on the water in the stream. She paused long enough to bathe her arms and feet, then crawled into the tent of Afraid-of-Birds and Standing Horse.

On the far side of the tepee, Crooked Feather was lying on his back, snoring lightly with his arms crossed over his chest. He had told her that in olden times, a boy his age would already be sleeping in a separate tepee for braves only and the girls would be staying with their parents. But in the Wild West show, things had gotten all mixed up, and boys slept with parents, and old men like Big Tree slept alone. She smiled and curled up beside the two small children. She was glad that the rules were all mixed up. It felt good to hear Crooked Feather's snoring.

That night Caroline dreamed she was lost in the woods. She moaned and tossed in her sleep as she struggled through briars and branches, looking for the path that would lead home. But when she finally saw the path, it was forked. Billy Big Tree and Dancing Rain and Crooked Feather stood in one path, beckoning her, while in the other path stood her smiling grandmother and her father.

13

Caroline spent every available moment helping Big Tree with chores—carrying wood or water to his tepee, starting his fire, washing his blanket, filling his pipe. He never seemed particularly glad to see her, and often he would sit in silence for many moments before speaking. Caroline learned, through trial and error, not to interrupt him as he told tales of his ancestors or the deities that lived all around them. Every stream, every rock, tree, animal was alive, according to Big Tree. Caroline thought it amazing.

"You mean a spirit lives in this old rock?" she teased, picking up a piece of limestone from the circle around the campfire.

"Everything in nature has value, even the most annoying insect and smelly fish."

"Hmm. Well, in that case, good evening, Mistress Rock," she said, and pretended to tip her hat to the stone. "I'm so sorry if I stepped on you yesterday. I surely didn't know you were a goddess." She giggled, but Big Tree did not laugh.

"You may mock our beliefs, but someday you may wish that you had not."

Then, as often happened, he fell into a long, complicated tale. Today's story concerned a boy who stepped on a stone one day and threw it away in anger. It lodged in a tree, and many years later, when he lay under the tree to take a nap, the stone fell free and hit him in the head, killing him.

After that lesson Caroline looked at rocks and trees and rivers and plants with a new respect, being careful not to show anger at any of them.

Obeying Big Tree's orders to "keep your eyes open and your mouth closed," Caroline began to learn words and phrases from the Wichita language. She thought it strange and beautiful at the same time and often mumbled sentences as she dozed off to sleep.

There were no other Wichita in the show. Indeed, according to Sam, there were only a few hundred Wichita left on the face of the earth. Big Tree never revealed to her how he came to be there, and no one else seemed to know, either. Most of the Indians were Sioux and Crow from the northern reservations. The rest were mostly Pawnee, Kiowa, Comanche, and Cheyenne from Indian Territory in the south.

Crooked Feather often joined Caroline in the cool of the evening as the old man told stories. More times than not, as Big Tree unveiled some episode with a straight face, Crooked Feather would burst out laughing.

"That's the funniest story I ever heard," he would say to Big Tree, while Caroline scratched her head and had not the slightest idea what he meant.

By the end of the second week in Indianapolis, Big Tree had accepted the fact that Caroline would visit him every morning and every night, and speak to him anytime she saw him. He never asked for her help, but she always gave it willingly. His tepee, a cluttered mess the first time Caroline had seen it, now looked neat and tidy inside.

"Big Tree," Caroline asked her grandfather one morning as she brushed and braided his long gray hair, "why don't you wear a big war-bonnet like the others? You're so old, surely you have earned enough feathers to reach the ground."

"War was not always the Wichita way of life. In the early times, our ancestors did not roam the plains searching for buffalo, except during the winters, when no corn would grow. In the spring and summer they farmed along the rivers. They lived in strong huts made of wood and thatched with grass. Brutal people, like the Osage and the Sioux, wanted our corn and made raids. They disdained us for being farmers. Our hunting men were forced to take up horses and become warriors to protect our villages. And once they had tasted the way of war, there was no turning back. My grandfather and my father before me were all peace chiefs. We selected the new places to camp and prayed for rain and healed those who were sick. After the White Man forced us to leave our tribal grounds and live in Indian Territory, there was no reason to have a peace chief or a war chief. I became useless and old."

"You're not useless, Grandfather. Why don't you make it rain now? There is a drought, and farmers are losing their crops. They would be eternally grateful for rain."

"I lost my powerful medicine many years ago. I have not brought rain since my daughter ran away."

"Was my mother born on the reservation or out on the prairie?"

As usual, when Caroline mentioned her mother, Big Tree grew quiet. He could not mention her name, so he referred to her simply as "the Girl."

"The Girl was born on the prairie and was as wild as the wind. One day the Girl sneaked to the place where the ponies were tied and climbed on the back of one, even though she was very young and was forbidden to ride. She rode at night, when she thought no one saw her, and learned to ride as well as a boy," Big Tree said in his singsong storyteller's voice.

"What about her family? Her mother? Her brothers and sisters? Where are they now?"

"They are all gone."

"None of them live in Indian Territory now?"

"No. The Girl was the only surviving child of an old man. Her two older brothers, filled with the courage and fire of youth, both died in battle, one with the Osage, the other with the White Man. The Girl's older sister and an aunt died during the long walk to the reservation in Indian Territory.

"The girl's mother, overcome with grief and loneliness for her lost home, and lacking the right herbs to cure herself or food to sustain herself, succumbed to disease during the first harsh winter on the reservation. Many died from starvation and sickness. Many others committed suicide rather than die that way.

"The Girl mourned her mother's passing for weeks and almost starved from loss of appetite. She carried out the duties of a faithful daughter and cared for her old father, whose heart was a rock in his chest. She still loved the ponies and rode when she could, for it was the one thing that freed her of her heavy burden.

"One day a white man came to the reservation looking for Indians to work in his Wild West show. He was not a famous man like Buffalo Bill or Pawnee Bill, but he gained permission from the Indian Agency to hire several men. The families of the men accompanied them.

"So the old father, seeing the sadness of his daughter and the futility of his people, and feeling useless to help them, agreed to go. For anyplace would be better than the reservation, with its walking ghosts and sad memories. He took the Girl, who had come of the age to find a husband, and they became part of the Wild West show.

"The Girl became an important star, riding her pony, doing tricks that any brave would envy. She began to associate with white men, and as she was beautiful and spirited, they admired her. Her old father warned her to avoid white men and their devious, untruthful ways, but she was young and trusting."

Every night for the next two days Caroline listened to the stories of her mother. On the third night, she curled up across the fire from Big Tree and listened to the final chapter of Dancing Rain's life.

"One day the Girl met a young man with yellow hair," Big Tree began after drawing smoke from his pipe. "She spent more time with him than with her old father. Her old father forbade her to see the white man, but she defied him and went to the tent of the young man and began to live with him. All month long, the show performed in Saint Louis. When the show packed up for another town, Yellow Hair said good-bye to the Girl and returned to his people. The Girl returned to her father's tent, broken-spirited and sad.

Months later, she confessed she was with child and had shamed him. She did not want to return to the reservation and begged her father to let her stay with him. But her old father's heart became a stone and he told her to leave him and go live with the white man. He told her she was not his daughter anymore for her betrayal. She took a horse and rode away. It was the last time the old father saw her."

Caroline's heart ached like a festering wound. "I think the Girl loved her old father very much," she whispered. "I think she forgave Old Father and would have returned to the reservation as soon as she could travel, but she died in childbirth. I think she spoke of Old Father when she was dying and asked for his forgiveness. And she wanted him to have her neckband." Caroline removed the beaded piece and handed it to Big Tree.

His frail, wrinkled fingers touched it for a moment, then he handed it back.

"No, I think the Girl wanted her neckband to go to her daughter as a token to remind the child of her mother's people."

So Caroline kept the neckband, and her heart grew fonder and fonder of the old man.

As the days passed in Indianapolis, Caroline learned how to sew beads and how to form intricate patterns from porcupine quills. She continued to save her nickels, dimes, and pennies and kept her eyes open for someone selling buckskin so she could make new clothes for her grandfather. But none was available.

"Why don't you make your own buckskin?" Crooked Feather suggested after hearing Caroline complain.

"I wouldn't know where to begin," she said. I don't even know what it's made from."

"Deerskin, of course."

"Can you teach me how to make buckskin?"

Crooked Feather grunted. "Tanning hides is women's work."

Caroline put her hands on her hips, struggling with her anger.

"I see. So tanning hides is women's work? And sewing clothes is women's work. And growing corn and cooking is women's work. Making the fires and setting up the tepees is women's work. What exactly is it that you men do?"

Crooked Feather scratched his chin a moment, then grinned.

"We hunt buffalo and deer. We steal horses and fight."

Caroline nodded. "That's what I thought. Well, there aren't any wars around here to fight, and no buffalo to hunt, so I guess you're of no use."

She brushed past him and returned to Afraid-of-Birds, who was busy starting a fresh fire.

"Where can I get deerskin for my grandfather's clothes?"

"Tell man to kill deer. I show you how to tan hide. Make buckskin," the woman replied in choppy English.

Caroline sighed as she left the tepee and walked toward the main arena. *Where can I get deer? We're in a city.* She climbed onto the grandstand and plopped down.

"Why so sad, little princess?" a familiar voice asked.

Caroline looked up into the face of Shawnee Sam, shaded by a wide-brimmed hat.

"I want something that cannot be," she said, resting her chin in her hands.

"Now, what kind of attitude is that? Where is your fighting spirit? I don't believe I'm hearing you give up. What is it you want?"

Caroline studied the face above her a moment, then straightened.

"I need some buckskin to make my grandfather a new ensemble. But to have buckskin I need deer. And we are in a town with no deer to hunt."

"A deer hunt?" Shawnee Sam stroked his blond beard, then his green eyes exploded with light.

"Little princess, you've just given me a brilliant idea—an actual deer hunt with live deer. It won't be as spectacular as Bill Cody's buffalo hunt, but the audience will love it. And then the skinning of the deer by the women, the tanning of the hides with brains—"

"Brains!" Caroline stood up.

"Of course, of course." Shawnee Sam

ignored her and continued to stare into space, lost in his idea.

"It could be a day-long event. A living tableau like the one at the Trans-Mississippi Exposition in Omaha two years ago. The first thing I have to do is find some deer. I don't want to kill the ones in the petting menagerie. They're not wild enough to give a good chase."

Caroline began to regret she had mentioned her problem, but it was too late. The idea had blossomed in Shawnee Sam's head and nothing could stop him. As with everything, he made a spectacular event out of it, and commissioned posters advertising that a deer hunt would be part of the Saturday morning show, followed by the skinning of the unfortunate animals, the tanning of the hides, and the construction of clothes.

The young Indian men did not seem to mind. They rallied at the idea of chasing live deer across the arena, and to make matters more interesting, Shawnee Sam had agreed to award the one to fell the first deer a bonus of twenty-five dollars.

When the day arrived, Caroline stared at the packed grandstand and hated herself for being the inspiration. The unfortunate deer, which had been captured earlier that week, were unloosed into the arena, where no less than a dozen young men, whooping and shouting, chased the frightened animals. The only one that Caroline truly knew was Crooked Feather, but she doubted that he would be the first to fell a deer. He himself admitted that he had spent most of his life in boarding school and had not yet mastered the bow and arrow.

Performers and audience alike had wagered on the outcome. The favorite was Red Hawk, a fierce Cheyenne brave about twenty years old, who wore a fantastic bone breastplate and whose bow was decorated with symbols of his coup victories.

The crowd cheered as the Indians chased the deer. On the sidelines, the older Indians complained about the disgraceful lack of sportsmanship and the disrespect to the deer. They shook their heads angrily and would have no part in the hunt.

By sheer coincidence, the first and second deer fell at the same instant, and to Caroline's surprise Crooked Feather's arrow was lodged in the heart of one of the lifeless animals.

Caroline smiled and applauded along with the audience and hoped Crooked Feather would win the money. But she had not read the handbills advertising the event and was taken completely by surprise when Shawnee Sam called her forward. She crossed the arena cautiously, apprehension creeping into her heart.

"Ladies and gentlemen," Sam shouted into the megaphone, "as you know, today's event was for the benefit of your favorite princess, Little Dancing Rain. For next week is her wedding day. And the young man who killed the first deer will be her husband."

Fury and fear rose in Caroline's heart like an angry grizzly bear and roared in her ears.

"No!" she whispered. "This is not possible!"

Shawnee Sam ignored her and continued with his spiel. "The princess, with the help of her mother and sisters, will skin the deer, tan it, and make her husband-to-be's wedding ensemble. This, of course, will take a few days, and will occur in the side tent. For only twenty-five cents you can watch the ongoing process.

"Now, Princess Little Dancing Rain, go meet your husband-to-be and accept his gift."

Caroline planted her feet in the soft ground, but Shawnee Sam was tall and strong and easily dragged her to the center of the arena. She saw the two deer lying limp and lifeless in the sand. The Cheyenne stood over his kill and Crooked Feather stood over his. Each youth's face registered its surprise as much as Caroline's, for Shawnee Sam had not mentioned the nature of his publicity stunt to them, either.

Shawnee Sam stopped in front of the two braves, then gently nudged each deer with his boot toe.

"We do have a slight problem," Sam announced after verifying the death of each deer. "I did not see which young brave killed the first deer. My friends tell me the animals fell at the same time. Which of these braves wins the prize of Princess Little Dancing Rain?"

Caroline imagined that her face was a shade of purple by now and she clenched her fists and gritted her teeth. How dare the old goat choose a husband for her, just for the benefit of the show? She would run away and go back to Aunt Oriona before she would consent to marry Red Hawk, with his fierce black eyes.

Everyone knew that the Cheyenne, of all the nations, hated white men the most. Even now, as Red Hawk glared at Shawnee Sam, his eyes seemed to simmer with hatred.

"Who shall win the princess?" Shawnee Sam reveled in the attention being poured over him by the enthralled audience. As Sam stepped around the two youths, he held his hand over each one's head and the audience cheered and hooted and shouted out the name of the man they wanted to win.

It was too close to call. Both youths were popular, Crooked Feather because of the snake dance and Red Hawk because of his prowess and exquisite costume.

Caroline saw Crooked Feather and Red Hawk whispering to each other and knew they were as embarrassed as she. It occurred to her, as Shawnee Sam turned his back on the two Indians and faced the audience, that it was quite a miracle that Sam had lived this long.

"How shall I choose? Another match of prowess? Bows and arrows? A footrace? A horse race?"

The crowd cheered or hissed as they fancied until one chant began to rise above the others. "Footrace! Footrace!"

Shawnee Sam held up his hand and grinned. "A footrace it is. Red Hawk and Crooked Feather, step to the end of the arena." Using the heel of his boot, Sam scratched a line in the sand at the opposite end. "The first one across this line wins the hand of the fair princess."

Caroline felt sick. She had seen Red Hawk race before. He was undefeatable. She stepped aside as Sam drew his pistol and fired it into the air.

In a flurry of feathers and beads and flying hair, the two youths raced toward the line. As she had expected, Red Hawk was far ahead of Crooked Feather, whose feet seemed to be stuck in the soft dirt. Suddenly Caroline heard her own voice shouting louder than any in the audience.

"Run, Crooked Feather! Run faster!"

As if taking her words to heart, Crooked Feather burst forward a few yards before the finish line and inched ahead of Red Hawk. As they flew past, Crooked Feather's right foot stepped on the line no more than two inches in front of his opponent's. Caroline heaved a sigh of relief. Her urge to throw her arms around Crooked Feather's sweaty neck was surpassed only by her urge to strike Shawnee Sam in the face. Crooked Feather said something to her, but she heard nothing because of the roaring crowd. Sam strutted around holding up Crooked Feather's hand as if he were a prize-fighter.

"Crooked Feather," he said at last, as the crowd grew quieter, "today you had very strong medicine. The Great Spirit blessed you. Now, meet your wife-to-be." Sam shoved Crooked Feather's wet, warm hand into Caroline's.

His hand squeezed hers and she glanced up at his flushed face. His dark eyes twinkled and his lips fought back a smile.

"We are *not* getting married," Caroline hissed under her breath. "This is only a gimmick for Sam's show."

"I know," Crooked Feather answered.

"I can't believe you beat Red Hawk. He's the fastest runner in the show."

"I know," Crooked Feather said, and once again the smile fought to be free.

"You were very lucky today."

"I know."

"How did you do it?"

Crooked Feather glanced at Caroline.

"You may not like the answer."

"Oh, I suppose you promised to give him the twenty-five-dollar prize money if he let you win." *At least that means you cared about me, and maybe that would be a kind of honor,* Caroline thought as she waited for his answer.

"Not exactly."

"Then how?"

Crooked Feather leaned closer and whispered into her ear.

"I told him the truth. I told him you were half-white and that you didn't know how to cook or clean or tan a deer hide or quill or bead and that his wedding ensemble would look ugly. He offered to pay me if I would let him lose the race honorably."

Caroline felt the heat rising to her ears; then she saw the smile spread across Crooked Feather's face and suddenly she could not hold her laughter back another moment.

For the next few days, Caroline, Afraid-of-Birds, and her sister became the center of attention in a side tent. Caroline watched the older women swiftly and expertly cut the deer's skin from its carcass. They showed her how to stake the pelt out and scrape the tissue off one side and the hair off the other. Then they removed the brains from the animals, mashed them into a paste, added water, and soaked the skins, squeezing and dipping several times until the material was soft and pliable. Then they stretched and pulled the skins over poles until the finished buckskin was velvety soft. Lastly they made a pit fire, and diverted light smoke over the skins to help make them resistant to water.

Even though the older women directed Caroline, she did most of the tedious work herself, and as she held the finished product in her hands, feeling the softness and smelling the sweetness, she had never felt prouder.

Shawnee Sam gave each of the women a small bonus for the extra work, but still Caroline held a grudge toward the tall man. She secretly swore to herself that she would never carry on a conversation with him again, in fear that something she might say would give him another "brilliant idea." And as the day for the final show approached—the one in which she and Crooked Feather would go through the motions of a wedding ceremony—dread filled her heart.

"Shawnee Sam," she said one day, "there is no possible way that I can finish this ensemble by the final day. Afraid-of-Birds is teaching me the art of beading and quilling, but I am slow and I have other duties to perform. I have to practice my trick riding and I have to help my grandfather with daily chores. Besides, as I told you from the beginning, the clothing is for my grandfather. How can I give it to Crooked Feather? They are not the same size."

"Oh, piddle," Sam said with a wave of his hand. "Those clothes always fit loosely. After Crooked Feather wears it during the ceremony, you can give it to your grandfather."

"No, I can't. That would be unthinkable. It would be an insult to both men." Caroline stomped her foot and crossed her arms. "I won't do it."

Shawnee Sam squinted and studied her face.

"By Jove, you do look familiar when you strike that pose. Are you sure you aren't related to the real Princess Dancing Rain?"

Caroline slowly unfolded her arms. "If I

tell you, will you promise to let Crooked Feather wear another costume and let me give this one to my grandfather?"

Shawnee Sam thought a moment, then nodded. "Agreed."

Caroline drew in a deep breath and expelled it slowly.

"The truth is, Dancing Rain was my mother."

"Thunderation! I thought she drowned in the river."

"No, she didn't."

"This is wondrous news. Is she alive, then?"

Caroline shook her head and glanced at the ground.

"No, sir. She died when I was born."

A look of desperate sadness swept over Sam's features and even his mustache seemed to droop.

"Oh, I'm so sorry. Who, might I ask, was your father?"

"Just a young roustabout in the show. A white man. That's all I know." Caroline decided to hold back some of the truth. After all, Sam had a notorious temper and there was no point bringing her father into the picture.

"I see. Then you truly are Billy's grand-daughter. I suspected as much when I couldn't find that fictitious grandfather's name you gave me. This is wonderful. Absolutely wonderful." He beamed and rubbed his hands together.

"Will you keep your promise?"

"Of course." He placed a gloved hand on her back and steered her toward the tepees.

As they passed his silk Arab-style tent, Sure Shot Sue stood in front of it, glaring at them.

"Let's keep this our secret, shall we?" he whispered. "There's no need for anyone else to know that you are only half-Indian. It might cause some problems with the authorities."

"That suits me fine," Caroline replied.

As she turned to go, Sam caught her arm and put his gloved hand on her chin, turning it sideways.

"Yes, of course. Why didn't I see it before now? You are the image of her. And you have her spirit. She was the most cantankerous girl at times, but very sweet and gentle at others. Everyone loved her. Everyone." He sighed, then straightened his hat. "Well, then, I shall just have to find Crooked Feather a different costume."

When Crooked Feather saw the costume

Shawnee Sam provided, apparently one bought from a Blackfoot shaman years ago, he threw a fit. Caroline's provided costume was an outlandish combination of several different tribal styles, including a fancy headdress with a real fox head on it. She and Crooked Feather felt foolish and tried not to laugh, for the show had to go on.

The final day in Indianapolis, a packed audience watched the mock wedding, thinking they were seeing a genuine Indian affair. Sam orchestrated the event, and in fact it had nothing in common with marriage rites of either the Wichita or the Kiowa—or any other Indian nation, for that matter.

All the Indians wore their finest clothing, decorated with every bead and feather and bell they could find. No matter what nation they belonged to, they took part in the ceremony. Drummers pounded the hollow tom-toms and the head singer led them in chorus after chorus of chants. The men's deep voices and the women's shrill ones blended into perfect harmony. Men and women alike swayed and lifted their feet in rhythm to the pounding drums. Shawnee Sam served as the master of ceremonies, speaking Pawnee—the Indian language he knew best—as he waved feathers over the heads of the young couple. In spite of her negative feelings about the ceremony, Caroline felt herself trembling with excitement as she held Crooked Feather's hand and repeated words after Sam. In the end, Sam told them to kiss, and she was sure that, like her, it was Crooked Feather's first encounter with the opposite sex, for his face blushed under the painted skin and his fingers shook.

After the ceremony, Caroline and Crooked Feather autographed and posed for photos for an endless stream of people. When the show finally closed for good, Caroline ripped off the feathered costume and consoled herself by counting her money.

That afternoon, after Shawnee Sam handed out the month's wages, Caroline hurried to town and bought several bags of colored beads and some colored ribbons.

Most of the performers, after receiving their wages, immediately filled the saloons and bordellos in the fair city of Indianapolis for the last time. Though the Indians were not supposed to drink alcohol, Caroline noticed that

Shawnee Sam turned his head the other way. And now the gambling games that many of the young braves and old chiefs had played for fun became games with real money. All night long they drank, and Shawnee Sam drank and gambled along with them. By the wee hours of the morning, he left with half the wages he had paid out back in his pockets.

Caroline tried to get Big Tree to leave the gambling tables, but to no avail. By the end of the night his wages were gone and his head was in a thick stupor from whiskey.

"You've gambled away all your money!" Caroline said angrily as she helped him stagger to his tepee.

"Money has no use," Big Tree replied. "All of White Man's money cannot bring back my wife and children. All of White Man's money cannot bring back the buffalo and the fields of corn and the way of my people. White Man's money cannot bring back the pride in my heart that I felt when I was young."

He waved Caroline aside and stumbled onto the prairie. He settled on the hard ground, wrapped his blanket around his skinny shoulders, and sat until he fell asleep.

The next day the roustabouts, complaining of hangovers and headaches, knocked down the tents and stands and temporary buildings. They loaded the train cars and soon the locomotive rolled onward to Cincinnati.

Caroline sat beside Crooked Feather in the back of the train, in the car assigned to Indians. At least *he* had not gambled away his wages; but he had purchased a new calico shirt and a black felt hat that made him look rather foolish, she thought.

Big Tree sat across from them, watching the countryside roll by. They passed field after field of withering cornstalks and puny wheat and dry creeks, for it had not rained during the entire month of May. Dairy cattle spotted the fields here and there, and farmhouses glistened in the sun.

"It is lovely, isn't it?" Caroline said as they passed over a creek that sweetly wandered through a pasture.

Big Tree snorted, then puffed on his pipe. He said something in his language that she did not understand.

She looked at Crooked Feather. "Well?"

"Big Tree says the land is ugly now that it

is fenced in. He remembers when herds of buffalo shook the earth like thunder. Their hooves spewed forth great clouds of dust that you could see for miles. And when they were peacefully grazing and you crept up on them, their number was so great it turned the green valleys brown."

Caroline sighed. "Maybe that's true, but look at all the lovely farms out there now. Nature is nice, but aren't people more important?"

Big Tree snorted again, then puffed his pipe.

"Sometimes I do not believe that you have one drop of Indian blood in your veins," Crooked Feather said, crossing his arms and pulling his new hat down low over his eyes.

Caroline glanced at Big Tree and felt the heat creeping up her cheeks.

"What does Billy Big Tree say to that?" Caroline asked, looking him in the eye.

For a response, he turned his face to the tiny window.

"The land is dying from a drought," he said to no one in particular.

Caroline nodded. At least they both agreed on that.

"I can see the corn shriveling, and the creek is low," she said. "The grass is dry and burnt black along the railroad tracks. Sparks from the train must have set it ablaze."

Caroline examined the fields again, more closely this time, and noticed that the earth was cracked into jagged shapes like pieces of a puzzle.

A long silence fell over the car, until at last Standing Horse, who sat across the aisle from Crooked Feather, spoke in the Kiowa language. Several Indians nodded in agreement.

"What did he say?" Caroline jabbed Crooked Feather, disturbing his rest.

"Standing Horse said that in the old days Big Tree would have danced and sung down the rain. He was renowned for his power even among those who were not Wichita. His magic made the rain clouds appear in a cloudless sky."

Big Tree stared out the window, watching the withered land go by. Caroline wondered if he was thinking of the old days when he danced and sang and worked magic from the cloudless sky. In every show, he pretended to be bringing the rain; the drums would rumble, and Shawnee Sam would come into the arena and beg Big Tree not to bring the rain, for it would make the good people in the audience get all wet. The audience would laugh and Shawnee Sam would pretend to speak to Big Tree in his own language, but he was really only saying gibberish. Then he would smile and tell everyone that Billy Big Tree would not bring the rain today.

Caroline had asked Sam once what he would do if by chance it really started to rain during Big Tree's act, and he said, "Why, I would tell the audience that Billy had brought it, of course. Either way, I can't lose."

As Caroline watched the thirsty cornstalks rolling by, she wondered what would happen if Sam let Big Tree finish his rain ceremony just once. With the land being so parched, maybe the audience wouldn't mind getting soaked.

And maybe it would give her grandfather back his pride.

14

It was Caroline's second grand procession parade and she loved it. Sitting atop Belle, she felt a rush of power. It was she the crowd cheered and waved at; it was she the children trembled at and hid from behind their mothers' skirts. She was as exotic to them as Big Tree had been to her that first time she saw him. Boys trotted alongside the procession, patting her pony's neck and withers, daring each other to touch Caroline's beaded moccasins. She ignored the boys, staring straight ahead unflinchingly, as she had seen Big Tree do so many times.

The sky over Cincinnati was clear blue and remained that way for the duration of the visit, with only an occasional light shower that did not stop the show. Caroline's act proved to be even more popular here than before. Her riding skills improved each day, and her legs and arms grew sinewy and strong. Crooked Feather taught her how to shoot a bow and arrow and gave her one to sling over her shoulder during the show. Caroline stitched a quiver to carry the arrows and added more beads and feathers to her costume. The other Indians began to accept her, and she no longer received their stares.

Caroline was not sure when she started speaking the Wichita language, but one night she suddenly realized that she understood most of what Big Tree was saying. From that day onward, she spoke to him in his own language as much as possible, using English only as a last resort.

Shawnee Sam's show brought in very little money in Cincinnati and he was anxious to go onward and fulfill his contracts in Columbus, Pittsburgh, Cleveland, Detroit, and Chicago. The final leg of the show would be two weeks in Omaha. Just when Caroline got used to the streets and buildings of Cincinnati it was time to pack and move on to Columbus. They passed the month of July in Pittsburgh and

Cleveland, then moved on to Detroit. They spent the last half of the hot, languid month of August in Chicago. Caroline and Crooked Feather had never seen so many people in one place, nor so many loud, rattling automobiles on the streets, frightening the horses and people.

As the days passed, Afraid-of-Birds diligently helped Caroline work on the new clothes for Big Tree in her spare time, and the finished product was far beyond Caroline's greatest imagination. Caroline didn't want her grandfather to know about the project, so she did the quilling and beading at night. Using her mother's neckband as a model, she meticulously strung beads and stitched them in the same pattern. She wanted to present the clothes to Big Tree on a special occasion, and waited for the right opportunity.

But with every day that passed, Caroline feared that right opportunity would never come. The whole region was still in the throes of the worst drought in memory. Not one good rain had blessed the land during the months that Caroline had been with the show. And though the autumn was normally the most lucrative time for the Wild West show, this year the farmers had lost their crops, cattle were dying of thirst and starvation, and everyone was economically stressed. Because of this, Shawnee Sam decided that a rain dance was no longer appropriate. After only one performance in Chicago, he had removed Big Tree from the program.

And with those orders began Billy Big Tree's downward spiral into oblivion. As long as he had been allowed to perform his dance and chant his song each day he'd seemed to have purpose. For though his rain dance had never been performed to completion, he'd had the respect of the other performers, and many had believed in him. Now his will to live plummeted, and he found no comfort, even in Caroline's daily visits. His stories became more tragic and dark and full of hopelessness.

"We are in the fourth era," he said to Caroline many times, but he would not explain to her what he meant.

Toward the end of the Chicago tour, when Sam assigned Big Tree to be one of the Indians massacred in the grand finale scene, the old man refused to cooperate. One day when he was supposed to play dead, he stood up and began dancing and chanting a death song around the people lying on the ground. When one of the women grabbed Big Tree's leg and tried to make him lie back down, he screamed as if he'd seen a ghost. The scene was intended to be serious and tragic, but the audience took it to be comedy and laughed. The second time it happened, a furious Shawnee Sam ordered Big Tree to stand on the sidelines and not take part in any of the acts.

The final ticket sales were a severe disappointment to Shawnee Sam. After the last day in Chicago, the roustabouts disassembled the show swiftly, with little celebrating. When they accidentally ripped a large hole in the main canopy, Sam did not even bother to have it repaired, claiming that they did not have to worry about rain. Everyone was in a foul mood, for their wages had to be cut and there was little hope that they would have a good showing at the final town of the season, Omaha.

September was still warm but at least the nights were cool, and the campfires inside the tepees felt cozy every evening. Caroline loved the quiet moments when she and Crooked

Feather sat on a blanket listening to Big Tree's wonderful stories, which transported her to another time and place.

In spite of Sam's orders to stay out of the show, one day Big Tree staggered into the arena in the middle of a cowboy's bulldogging act and started his rain dance and his chanting. The bull was not very happy and charged at Big Tree, who narrowly missed being gored. He fell on his face in the sand, and one of the cowboys had to rope the steer. The small audience hissed and booed as Caroline ran to her grandfather and helped him to the back lot.

Ill-tempered and frustrated because of the poor audience attendance, Shawnee Sam threatened to send Big Tree back to Indian Territory immediately.

"Please don't send him back," Caroline pleaded with all her heart. "He's just old and forgetful. If you had just let him keep on performing his rain dance, none of this would have happened."

Shawnee Sam glared at Caroline, and then at Big Tree, who was chanting softly as he stared at the horizon.

"I explained to you and him that the audience doesn't appreciate me stopping a rain dance with this drought killing off livestock and crops."

"Then let Big Tree finish his dance for once. Maybe it really will rain. The old Indians say he can make it rain if he wants to."

Shawnee Sam tilted his head back and roared. "If I thought he could do that, I would charge the farmers in Nebraska and Iowa fifty dollars a ticket, then retire for life."

At that moment Big Tree stopped chanting. A bit of fire exploded in his eyes and his grip on his rattle tightened.

"Can you bring the rain to this parched land?" Caroline asked her grandfather in his own language.

"It would take many days of preparation and sacrifice. I would need help," he responded.

Caroline quickly translated for Sam, who scratched his chin.

"It would make a good grand finale show, wouldn't it?" Caroline suggested. "The newspaper headlines could read 'Indian Rainmaker Brings Rain as a Gesture of Friendship for His White Friends.'" Caroline hated herself for once again scheming with Sam, but this time it was a matter of life and death.

"I could prepare some special handbills," Sam said, his eyes all dreamy and staring off into space like they did when he was thinking of a new act. "If I pull it off, the farmers will flock from every county to see this rain dance. I could have Billy do his preparations for several days, and then put off the actual dance until the last performance."

"And if it was the last show of the season, and the last act of the show, what would it matter if it didn't rain? You would leave the next day anyhow."

Shawnee Sam's green eyes twinkled. "All right, then. I will allow Billy to perform one final rain dance, and I promise I won't stop his act. I'll advertise and make it the most attended show in history. Tell Billy to buy whatever he needs for the final day, one week from now. But by Jove, if he spoils one more performance before then, I'll take his wages out of yours. Do you understand?"

Caroline shook Sam's glove-covered hand, then took Big Tree by the elbow and led him to his tepee.

"Shawnee Sam wants you to perform a real rain dance on the last day of the season. He wants you to make it rain, really rain. Whatever you need, I will get for you."

Big Tree stared out the tepee flaps at the cloudless sky.

"Will you do it, Grandfather?"

"It is a sacred ceremony. There must be much sacrificing."

"What kind of sacrificing?"

"I cannot eat or sleep. I must purify my body and sing and dance and say sacred prayers. I will need special river rocks."

"I'll take you to the river and gather some."

"I will need feathers from songbirds."

"Crooked Feather will get them for you."

"I will need live frogs to help me sing."

"There are plenty of them by the river."

"Then it will be done."

"But you must agree not to interfere with the other acts until then. Shawnee Sam is very angry and will send you back to Indian Territory."

"I have no life there. I have no life here."

"You do have a life, Grandfather. And I will take care of you no matter where you live."

"I will bring down the rain. It will be my parting gift to the White Man to repay him for all he has done for my people."

Caroline hugged Big Tree's bony shoulders and helped him settle into his bed. It was like lifting a bag of feathers, so frail was his body.

He slept well that night and awoke early. He was a new man, with purpose in his step. He and Caroline, as well as Crooked Feather and Afraid-of-Birds, walked to the river and selected special stones, then caught a few frogs and, with great effort, snared some songbirds.

Big Tree built a small grass hut, and four days before the final performance he filled it with stones that had been cooked in a fire for hours. He threw water on the stones and a great hissing steam filled the hut, penetrating the pores of his naked body. After singing prayers, he carried his wrinkled body to a nearby stream and splashed in the cool water.

Soon afterward he boiled yaupon leaves until the liquid turned black. After drinking the smelly liquid, he vomited until his insides had been purged.

Caroline presented him with the new

clothes that she had worked on so diligently for weeks. They hung a bit too loosely on his thin frame, but he had never looked more handsome to her. Big Tree accepted the clothes quietly and wore them proudly, even complimenting her on the beadwork and quilling. Caroline combed and braided his long gray hair and put raven feathers in it.

Weak and shaky, he scratched a circle near a field of dying corn. In the center he placed a rain bundle, made with cedar and feathers of the songbirds, and an ear of corn.

As each day passed, Caroline's heart filled with remorse at his failing health and she dared not leave the old man, except when she had to perform her act. Crooked Feather brought bedding and built a fire beside the old man. He stayed with Caroline, curled up beside the fire, every night. All the Indians in the show came to pay their respects to Billy Big Tree, laying at his feet gifts and food for when the ceremony was over. Mothers let their children touch the old wrinkled body for good luck.

"I wish I had never suggested the rain dance," Caroline whispered to Crooked Feather on the third night. "Look how pale and weak Big Tree is. And the sky is just as cloudless as when he started. What happens to him if he cannot bring the rain?"

"You must have faith or your doubting thoughts will rise to Heaven and destroy your grandfather's prayers."

"Do you believe he will bring rain?"

"Yes. And so do all the other Indians. All our hearts are praying with him. We know he will succeed."

"But he is so old and weak. He needs nourishment or he will die."

Crooked Feather turned to Caroline, leaning on his elbow. "I thought you understood that this ceremony requires sacrifice."

"I didn't know he would sacrifice this much. I thought maybe a bath in cold water, or a day or two without food, or killing a frog or something of that nature. But this...this is cruel. He hasn't eaten food in three days and only drinks water once a day. And he has danced and chanted himself into exhaustion. I cannot stand by and watch him suffer just because I wanted something."

"Your heart was good. You wanted him to be proud again."

"No, no. All my motives were selfish. I wanted to be proud of him, to prove to all those laughing critics that he was the greatest rain-maker of them all. I wanted to boast about his talents and glow in the praise he would receive. I wanted it for me, too, not just for him."

"You must not feel that way, Caroline. His sacrifice is not for you," Crooked Feather said, nudging her arm. "He has felt great shame because of his actions, because of his life. He is doing the rain ceremony to redeem himself among his people and his gods."

"Redeem himself for what?"

"For leaving his people on the reservation many years ago. For sending his daughter away to die. For embarrassing himself in front of the White Man's audience."

"So if he brings the rain, he will be re-deemed? Good, then he and I can get back to our lives."

"When he brings the rain, he will be re-deemed in the eyes of his people, but you will not return to a normal life."

"What do you mean?"

"He will bring rain, but he will surely die. That is the ultimate sacrifice he must make. All the great rainmakers must be willing to give their lives to save the people. It is part of this ceremony."

A sudden sickness passed over Caroline. Her grandfather, whom she had found so short a time ago, was now going to die. All because of her selfish desires.

15

The chanting and dancing continued night and day, until Big Tree was too exhausted to dance. After that he sat cross-legged and chanted in rhythm to the drum and the bells on his turtle-shell rattle. Each time Caroline brought him food, he refused to take it, so she sat and listened to the stories of his people—of prankster animals and wise animals, of brave men and kind women.

On the final night, in low, deliberate tones, he told her the story of the creation of his people.

"There are four eras of mankind. In the first era the world appeared one day as land floating on water. First Man and First Woman were created and given corn and bows and arrows. But the world was in darkness and remained that way until First Man slew three deer. When the deer were slain, daylight flooded the world, and villages full of people and fields and forests full of animals suddenly appeared. First Man and First Woman traveled from village to village, teaching the people how to be good and how to conduct themselves. When this task was done and all the people knew what they were supposed to do, First Man became Morning Star, and First Woman became Bright Shining Woman, the moon.

"In the second era, the people scattered all over the earth. They named themselves many different names and some turned into the animals whose names they had taken. It was an era of wrongdoing, and many forgot their duties, as did the animals and even the deities in the skies. At the end of the era, a woman gave birth to four monsters, whose heads arched to the sky. To destroy the monsters and the wrong and willful world, a great deluge was sent.

"One man and one woman survived the flood. Once again they were given an ear of corn and bows and arrows. The gods taught them many skills, including how to construct a grass lodge. They taught their children about the ancient world. Animals gave their powers and their secrets to the children, who dutifully carried out the dieties' instructions. They were told that they would die; but one person who had died returned from Spirit Land, so they learned of the other world, and learned of life after death.

"In the fourth era, the world will end. The end is fast approaching us now. Needful things will no longer be provided; people will no longer be able to get things done. Weeds will grow in place of corn. Animals, trees, and running water will talk to men. Incest will occur and no more children will be born and all people will lose their good judgment. Animals will fail to procreate, and in the end the world will become uninhabitable. But just before the end, a great star in Heaven will select an important man to explain to the people what is happening. All the stars and the sun will become human again, as in the beginning of time, and the four eras will begin once more."

The fourth day of the ceremony, which was a Saturday, dawned with a sky as blue and cloudless as before. The last show of the day was that afternoon, and the crowd was immense. Everyone knew it was Shawnee Sam's last show not only in this town but for the season. Those who had missed the show before scampered to buy tickets. The newspapers had been covering the story of Billy Big Tree's rain dance, and it was drawing large crowds. Many people walked to the cornfield to watch Big Tree chanting and shaking his rattle. Caroline wanted to shoo them away like annoying crows, but Shawnee Sam made it clear that Big Tree was still part of the Wild West show, even though he was not in the arena.

Just before the last show, Shawnee Sam sent two roustabouts to bring Big Tree to the main arena. They had to carry him on a litter, so great was his weakness. They plopped him in the dirt in a far corner of the arena. Caroline silently placed the sacred objects in the circle around him and straightened his clothing. His voice was hardly more than a hoarse whisper as he chanted.

"Grandfather," she said to him, "you must eat and drink or you will die."

"I am ready to die. I have lived too long. An old man is weak and useless. If I bring rain, I will have served a purpose."

"You're not useless to me. I want to take care of you. When I turn eighteen I will inherit a lot of wealth. I'll buy some land on the prairie and you can build a grass lodge and bring all our people to live and grow corn and hunt buffalo. It will be like the old days, when you were a young man. You can teach children about the four eras, and about Morning Star and Bright Shining Woman. You can teach them everything they need to know to survive. You are not useless."

For a reply, Big Tree took up the rain bundles and the rattle again and began to chant.

That afternoon, Caroline performed her act without thinking or knowing what she did. The audience cheered and applauded, but she did not notice. She only had eyes for her grandfather, whose hoarse voice and weak rattle could not be heard above the band's music, and the thundering hooves, and the audience's applause.

After her performance, Caroline returned to Big Tree and sat beside him. His forehead was hot and feverish. She wiped his face with a red bandanna dipped in cool water.

One time Shawnee Sam rode over and looked at Big Tree, then looked up at the blue sky. He had discarded the canopy today, with canvas only covering the crowded grandstand and stretching around the outer perimeter of the arena.

"I don't see any rain clouds," Sam said.

"Don't worry, it will rain!" Caroline shouted up at him.

About halfway through the show, the audience began to boo and hiss Big Tree. Some threw trash at him. Why they took it upon themselves to show such cruelty to an old man, Caroline could not understand. Big Tree ignored them, but the fury rose to Caroline's cheeks. She leaped on her horse and rode around the arena, shouting at the crowd and brandishing her bow. She picked up bits of trash and threw them back at the audience until Shawnee Sam hurried out and told her to sit back down or be removed by force. The crowd no doubt thought that all this was part of the show, for many of them clapped when Caroline took a swing at Sam and almost knocked him from his horse.

Big Tree seemed to know that the grand finale was approaching. He managed to collect enough strength to rise to his feet and shuffle around the circle one final time. His voice grew lower and his drumbeat grew stronger, a sure sign that the end of the dance was approaching.

How ironic it was, Caroline thought, that the first rain clouds appeared during the act depicting the massacre of the Indians. She faithfully enacted her role, along with Afraid-of-Birds and her children. As they lay down pretending to be dead, a big drop of water hit Caroline's face. At first she thought it was only sweat from one of the braves dancing nearby, or perhaps a speck of paint from their decorated faces and ponies.

But as the Indians rode out into the hippodrome to attack the cavalry, there was no mistake. Thunder rocked the sky and shook the bleachers. The crowd screamed. Several men ran down the bleachers and out of the arena to get a better look. They ran back inside, shouting to the crowd.

"Rain clouds in the northwest. Big black ones!"

Men began evacuating the stands in a frenzy to better see the clouds. The women and children who stayed behind muttered and mumbled among themselves.

As another rumble of thunder rocked the earth, Big Tree staggered and collapsed.

"Grandfather!" Caroline screamed, and though she was supposed to be dead, she ran across the arena. Crooked Feather rode beside her long enough to swoop her up onto his horse. He gently dropped her beside Big Tree and dismounted.

In spite of the disturbance, the enactment of Custer's Last Charge continued, and as the band broke into a raging tune of fury, the drops fell faster and faster. Now the sky was black where once it had been blue. The audience cheered and went wild, shouting and waving, clasping hands and dancing.

Lightning streaked across the sky, and as if by a signal, the clouds opened up and the rain fell in thick gray waves. The wind whistled through the stands, tugging at the ropes and flapping the canvas like a rooster would flap its wings.

With a loud peal of thunder and a simultaneous crack of lightning, ropes gave way and the canvas tore free, exposing the audience. Everyone screamed and scattered for cover.

Caroline threw her arms around Big Tree, laughing and smiling. Crooked Feather, drenched and smelling of wet buckskin and wet feathers, started to lift Big Tree into his arms.

"I'll carry him to his tepee."

"No," Big Tree whispered, and held his hand up. "I want to feel the rain on my face. It has been too, too long since the rain has purified my soul."

Caroline helped her grandfather into a sitting position, her arms wrapped around his skinny shoulders, trying to protect him from the deluge.

"You are the greatest rainmaker in the world, Grandfather. Now no one will laugh at Billy Big Tree again. They all respect you. You can leave the show and come live with me. I will take care of you."

Big Tree looked into her face. He spoke slowly, deliberately.

"My daughter loved the rain. She would dance and sing. That's why we called her

Dancing Rain. You have her heart and her spirit. I see her eyes and her face when I look at you, and I know she lives on. That is good."

His old fingers touched Caroline's cheeks for the first time since they had met.

"Let us take you inside away from the storm," Crooked Feather said gently. "We do not want you to get sick."

But Big Tree shook his head. "My work is done. I have repaid all my debts, and it is time to join my ancestors." As Big Tree spoke his weary eyes brightened and a smile touched his lips.

He began to sing his own death song in a hoarse voice:

"I see my father now. He says I have lingered here on earth too long, like I always lingered at the river too long. My wife is telling me to hurry home or I will miss my supper of corn and beans and sweet venison. My daughters are saying that the water is clear and sweet. My sons are saying that the grass is green and the buffalo herd never ends. I am home at last."

With those words, he closed his eyes and breathed no more. His brow, always furrowed with worry and sadness, grew smooth, and an expression of peace enveloped the wrinkled face.

"Good-bye, Grandfather," Caroline said, and kissed his damp cheek.

Caroline felt a great emptiness in her heart, just as she had the day her grandmother died. She rested her cheek on the old man's motionless chest for a moment and let her tears stream down her face, only to be washed away by the rain.

After a moment, Caroline felt a hand gently touch her shoulder. She looked up into Crooked Feather's face. She could not tell if he was crying, because of the rain; but his dark eyes were full of gentleness and she suddenly wanted to throw her arms around him and hug him with all her might. But she knew he would not approve of such a display of emotion. It was not the way of his people.

"I hardly found my grandfather, and now he's gone," she said in disbelief. "He just as good as killed himself with this rain ceremony. Why did he do it? Surely not for the White Man who caused him so much pain?"

"Don't you know why?"

Caroline drew in a deep breath and let it

out slowly. "Yes, I guess I do. He did it to regain respect. He used to say, 'A man without respect and honor is no more than the skin of a man with nothing inside.' He would rather die with honor than live without it."

"He is in a far better place than this," Crooked Feather said as he pointed to the arena. Caroline thought she heard a sigh of envy escape from his lips. "I think it is time to go inside, out of the rain. Do you want me to make arrangements for the burial ceremony?"

Caroline nodded. "Yes. Do you think he would like to be buried on that hill over there, under that oak tree overlooking the river? He told me that it was the custom of the Wichita to bury the dead on a hill."

Crooked Feather nodded. "You knew him well."

"Not nearly well enough," she replied.

Crooked Feather carried Billy Big Tree inside the main performers' tent, where everyone was singing and dancing and fiddles were playing merry tunes. Even Sure Shot Sue and Shawnee Sam were dancing a jig.

When they saw Crooked Feather's precious burden, they grew silent. The cowboys removed their hats, and the Indians hung their heads sadly.

Afraid-of-Birds helped Caroline wash her grandfather's body and braid his hair while the men went off to dig a grave. The Indians, though of many different nations, sang and danced and beat the drums. All the while the rain continued to fall in torrents.

Caroline placed her grandfather's favorite pipe in his callused hands, along with his medicine pouch and sacred stones, and turned his face toward the east. Lastly, she placed the poster of her mother beside him. While Lost Wolf, the oldest man there, sang a farewell song, Caroline and a somber Shawnee Sam whispered the Lord's Prayer.

It seemed like only yesterday that she had stood over her grandmother's grave and whispered the same words. Once again her heart throbbed with pain and sorrow.

After the ceremony, Shawnee Sam, his face long and sad, wrapped one arm around Caroline and held an umbrella over her with his free hand.

"I'm sorry about your grandfather. I truly admired that old man."

"Thank you, sir."

"What will you do now? Big Tree had no relatives left in Indian Territory."

Caroline felt a shiver and she shrugged.

"I don't know what will happen. I guess I—" She sighed. "I just don't know."

"I hope you'll consider being in my show next year. You're a great talent and the audiences love you."

"I don't know..."

"Perhaps I can help you make up your mind. As you may know, Sue and I never had children. I would be honored to adopt you as my daughter. You could live with us in Saint Louis. We have a very respectable house. Not a tom-tom or tepee or cowboy in sight, I promise you." He chuckled. "What do you say?"

Caroline stared at his sincere face, too shocked to reply.

"Why me, sir? There are hundreds of orphans in the country. I hear they ship them by the trainload out west."

"To be truthful, I cared about your mother very much. I guess you could say I loved her. If things had been different, I might have been your father and she would still be alive. But I had already married Sue and, well, the Lord had something else in store for you, I guess."

"Sue doesn't like me," Caroline said at last, as his words finally sank in.

He smiled. "Sue doesn't like anybody. That doesn't matter, does it? Won't you at least think about it?"

Caroline nodded and watched the tall man stride away, his long hair clinging to his neck in blond ringlets. In spite of his annoying ways, she felt a twinge of pride that he wanted her as a daughter. She could do far worse for a father. Far worse.

When Caroline arrived back at Standing Horse's tepee, she didn't want to think about anything, so she curled up on a buffalo robe and fell into a deep sleep.

The rain continued to fall all the next day, and the next. Shawnee Sam had delayed packing up, hoping the rain would stop; but when it became evident there was no letup, the roustabouts grumbled and broke down the equipment in the pouring rain. The Indian women scurried to disassemble the tepees and load them onto the train. The wagons got stuck in the mud, causing Shawnee Sam to grow irritable, and every other word that left his lips was a curse on the once-precious rain.

By the third day, Shawnee Sam's Wild West show was on the train heading to Saint Louis, hoping for drier ground. Since Omaha had been the last show of the season, Sam paid the cowboys, vaqueros, and sharpshooters, and they dispersed to all corners. Shawnee Sam's righthand man rode north with the Indians who had come from the northern reservations. The other Indians, including Crooked Feather and Standing Horse's family, climbed aboard the southward-bound train, which would take them back to Indian Territory.

The creeks burst over their banks and the river roared, swallowing up houses and entire sections of the town. Many devastated families packed their belongings onto wagons, but they could not escape, for all the roads were under water and the mud was two feet deep in many places.

The fields of corn and wheat, already dead from drought, stood in silver sheets of water. Waterfowl squawked in the fields where once crows cawed.

In the last car Caroline sat beside Crooked Feather as the train chugged southward at a snail's pace. She pressed her face to the window, its once-sooty surface washed clean by the pouring rain. Afraid-of-Birds was pale and silent and clung to her children, as did all the women. Tension prickled the air and even the usual card games had been suspended.

"It is unwise to send the train out in this rain," Standing Horse finally said, breaking the silence.

"I saw a cow swimming," Afraid-of-Birds remarked to no one in particular.

"I saw a cow in a tree," said her sister.

"She must have been blinded by the rain and stepped off a bluff," someone explained.

The conversations continued like that, short remarks about cows and the weather and the cornfields.

While everyone else wondered if the fields in Indian Territory were also being drowned by rain, Caroline thought about her future. When she ran away from her cousin Mattie's house, she'd had no further thought in her head than to find out about her mother and discover if she had any living relatives. Once she had met Billy

Big Tree and learned to love the old man, she'd thought she would live with him in Indian Territory and take care of him for the rest of his life. No one in her family knew what had happened to Caroline. Perhaps they thought she had been killed or stolen away. Obviously they had not thought of the Wild West show or her father would have tracked her down. Now she did not know what to do.

Living with Shawnee Sam had much appeal; surely she would become the star of the show and be allowed to perform any act within a few years. But the thought of facing Sure Shot Sue and her whiskey bottle every day dampened Caroline's enthusiasm for that idea. Aunt Oriona would probably forgive her and take her back. So would Mattie, for the right amount of money. And, of course, there was her father.

Caroline pressed her fingers into her temples and tried to banish the image of Jackson Long selling her beloved horse to a stranger and putting her on the train, and the image of Jackson Long searching door-to-door in the boardinghouse to find her so he could receive his pieces of silver.

Caroline studied each choice thoroughly,

imagining the best and worst things possible. She no longer felt welcome at Mattie's house, she still felt hated by Aunt Oriona, and no matter where she went, Jackson would no doubt try to persuade her to part with her inheritance at every chance.

Caroline glanced at Crooked Feather. His head was slumped on his chest and his black hat with the red feather was pulled down low over his brow. He had not invited Caroline to go to Indian Territory with him, nor had Standing Horse or Afraid-of-Birds. In spite of the mock wedding ceremony and all they had been through, Caroline still did not know Crooked Feather's heart.

By the time the train had pushed a few miles outside of the town, Caroline's head was churning so fiercely with indecision that she wanted to scream. She stood up and walked to the door.

Dirty water spewed out from the wheels in brown sheets as the train sped over the tracks. Up ahead she saw a bridge over a creek. The creek, probably once small and tame, now roared like an angry brown serpent.

Suddenly a loud crunching noise and the

screech of brakes filled the air. Caroline felt the train lurch, and before she could grab anything, she was on her stomach sliding across the floor. The crunching and squealing, and the horrible cries of cows and horses and humans, continued for several seconds. Caroline squeezed her eyes shut as she clung to the nearest seat frame for dear life.

She heard a noise and looked up to see Crooked Feather stumbling toward her on unsteady feet. He collapsed by her side and wrapped his arms around her. She clung to him, feeling his heart pounding like a drum. From the front of the train, shrieks of panic and terror filled the air.

After the train finally stopped, Crooked Feather helped Caroline up. The Indians scrambled out of the last car and stood in the muddy field, gasping at what they saw. The rails and ties had washed away in front of the bridge, and the engine and first two cars of the train had tumbled into the creek. The next three cars lay on their sides, broken into mangled piles of splintered wood and metal. Horses and cattle had scattered free.

For the first time in a generation, buffalo

were racing across the prairie. The tired old cow snorted the fresh air, then charged like a playful calf with her tail twisting and her heels kicking.

While some of the cowboys got out their ropes and rounded up horses to ride to town for help, Caroline and the Indians pulled the wounded from the wreckage. The last car, the one assigned to the Indians because of its discomfort, had not been damaged, and none of the Indians had been hurt.

Caroline walked among the dead and dying, helping those she could, saying a quick prayer over those she could not. She saw the distinctive buckskin coat of Sure Shot Sue, then saw the plump woman crushed lifeless by a heavy mahogany liquor bar that Sue had purchased for their expensive home in Saint Louis. A few feet away Shawnee Sam moaned, his torso crushed and trapped beneath some heavy furniture. Caroline ran to him and knelt. There was nothing she could do. As she wiped the blood from his eyes, he took her hand and squeezed weakly.

"It's their revenge... because of the buffalo," he said in a pained voice. "Tell them I'm sorry about the buffalo." His voice trailed to a whisper, then his breathing stopped.

Caroline folded his arms over his motionless chest and closed his eyelids.

By the end of the day, the dead had been carried to town and the wounded treated. The Indians had captured their horses and strapped all their belongings onto the saddles and travois.

Caroline had felt an empty hole in her chest with the death of Big Tree, and now the death of Shawnee Sam weighted her down even more. She had no one left to turn to.

"What will you do? Go to Indian Territory?" Crooked Feather said as he snugly tied the rawhide padding around his pony's back. The rain had stopped shortly after the train wreck, and sunlight now streaked through the clouds.

"I have no family there, now that Big Tree is gone."

"Have you forgotten what I told you? There are no orphans in an Indian village."

"Everyone will know I am part white."

"But part of you is not. You must choose. You can only be one or the other; you cannot be both."

"That's what Big Tree said, but I'm not so sure I agree with that. I do not know which part of me to follow, but I know that I am stronger for having both. But you sound as if you've made up your mind, Crooked Feather."

He nodded. "I attended White Man's schools and learned White Man's religion. I did everything I was taught to become a good Indian, but when I tried to live in the White Man's world, I was no more accepted than I had been when I was a papoose strapped to my mother's back. If anything, I was scorned more, and despised by White Man for trying to imitate him. I was seen as weak and spineless. The ones who slew White Man are more respected than those of us who tried to accommodate him."

"Then what will you do?"

"I'm returning to live with my uncles."

"But you said your family and the other Indians do not accept you and your educated friends—you are a Lost Child, remember?"

"Then I will have to start over. I will have to learn how to be an Indian. I will have to be taught to hunt and sing sacred songs and dance sacred dances. I will have to be taught the stories of my ancestors and the ways of my people before it is too late. Already the government orders us to abandon our Indian customs. But I will be a student of my own people and write our ways down on paper so they will never be forgotten. Then maybe my people will accept me."

"I am happy for you, Crooked Feather. You are a true friend."

"Will you come with me? Afraid-of-Birds will take you in like a daughter. We can ride the hills together. I can show you all the secret places I remember from my childhood. Perhaps we can have a true wedding ceremony someday."

Caroline thought about the wide open spaces. She imagined the feel of the wind blowing in her hair as she rode a spotted pony across the plain.

For a long moment her heart soared at the thought of saying yes, of living the rest of her life with Crooked Feather. Maybe they would get married, have children. And in another generation, all but a few drops of her father's blood would be gone.

She parted her lips to reply, but suddenly she imagined Grandmother Long's sweet face.

Everything Caroline had learned about being good and kind had come from that gentle woman. And she thought about Mattie, high-spirited and self-sufficient and determined to change the world for women. And she thought of her father, the softness of his blond hair, the warmth of his hugs. She had loved him with all her childish heart once. Surely he had some goodness buried beneath the veneer of selfishness.

Caroline sighed.

"I promise that someday I will come to Indian Territory, Crooked Feather, but not yet. I have too many unanswered questions and too much unfinished business. You know, Billy Big Tree used to say that every story changes according to the man telling it. That the same story told by one man might be sad and by a different man might be funny. He said that life is like that, too—your life is a story that changes over the years. When I was little, my story was being told by Grandmother Long, a kind, gentle woman, and I was happy. When she died, my Aunt Oriona began telling my story, and it was full of pain and torture. And when Billy Big Tree took over, my life changed into something mystical and wonderful. I'm fourteen now, and almost a grown woman. It's about time I took over my life story for myself and got it back on the right path."

Caroline extended her hands to Crooked Feather. He clasped them firmly with his own, then made the sign of peace and rode away.

16

It was years before Caroline kept her promise. After the train wreck, she used the money she had earned in Shawnee Sam's show to pay for a ticket to Saint Louis, where she worked as a chore girl in a boardinghouse in exchange for free room and board and earned extra money giving piano lessons. She occasionally saw Mattie, who had married into wealth and now had romping twin boys. But they never became close friends again, and Caroline always felt that Mattie did not want her in-laws to know that Caroline was part Indian.

When Caroline turned eighteen, she returned to the little Missouri river town to collect her inheritance. Aunt Oriona was old and dying and seemed genuinely happy to find out that Caroline was alive and well. Caroline found it easy to forgive the lonely, white-haired woman and had her buried next to Grandmother Long.

Caroline learned that her father had died in a New Orleans gambling house, broken and penniless, not long after she had run away. In spite of his selfishness, Caroline cried for days at the news. She took flowers to his grave every Sunday.

She also had a fine granite headstone erected over a sad, lonely grave, which was far removed from the family plot. All her life Caroline had seen the border of white rocks marking the grave's boundaries, but not until Aunt Oriona lay on her deathbed did she tell Caroline that the mound of earth was Dancing Rain's final resting place.

After Aunt Oriona's death, Caroline did not stay in the white clapboard house with the green shutters. She left Joshua, Ester, and newly married Taffy in charge of the house while she attended college. She was the first woman to graduate from her college's hallowed gates, and without doubt the first Indian to grace its halls.

For two years Caroline taught music and literature at a renowned boys' school, then one day a terrible rainstorm swept across the campus, causing an early dismissal of classes. As Caroline listened to the thunder and let the rain caress her face, something came over her. The next day she gave notice of her intent to resign. A month later she packed her belongings and purchased a train ticket for the newly formed state of Oklahoma.

Caroline stepped from the train and gazed at the open fields and hills dotted with cattle and horses. She filled her lungs with the fresh sweet air and strode to the Indian Agency office, suitcase in hand.

"Miss Long," the agent said, rising to his feet and removing his hat in the most gentlemanly fashion. "We're so pleased to have you here. The children are eager to meet their new teacher."

"And I am eager to meet my students," Caroline replied. She kept her hand on her straw hat as they walked across the dirt road to a small, dirty building in need of a lot of repairs.

"Why is this building in such poor condition, Mr. Boyles?"

He shrugged. "You'll learn that the Indians don't care much for education. It's hard enough to get the children to come here, much less learn their ABCs and numbers. You won't get much cooperation. You know, they're a lazy breed of people and don't think highly of White Men's ways."

"Is that so?" Caroline replied.

The first day of school, Caroline discarded her prim blue dress with its white lace collar and removed her high-top buttoned shoes. She unpacked her mother's neckband and the buckskin clothing of long ago, recently altered to fit her woman's body. She stood at the door of the wooden school building, ringing the bell. When no one came, she took a walk among the nearest squalid buildings, ringing the bell again. When the children still did not come out, she borrowed a horse and rode in circles, shifting around the saddle, riding backward, and swooping down to grab a bucket from the ground. A group of children came out, smiling and laughing.

The next day, when Caroline rang the bell,

the schoolhouse overflowed with children and their parents. A handsome young man holding the hand of a small boy stood in the doorway.

"You kept your promise," the man said.

"I beg your pardon?"

"Doesn't Princess Little Dancing Rain remember me?"

Caroline's heart soared with joy, but she did not throw her arms around the man's neck as she wanted to. Instead, she smiled at the little boy with big eyes. He looked exactly like Crooked Feather.

"Of course I kept my promise. I was taught by a very great man to always keep my word." She glanced at the child. "Your son?"

Crooked Feather nodded.

"Only one child?"

"Yes. My wife died giving birth."

"Oh." Caroline felt a jab of pain. "I'm very sorry."

"And you? Did you marry?"

Caroline shook her head. "That chapter in my life's story has not been told yet." She glanced at Crooked Feather for a sign of reaction, but his expression was hard and emotionless.

"Why did you come here, Caroline? Are

you here to teach our children White Man's history and White Man's religion? Are you going to teach my son that Indian ways are wrong and that White Man's ways are right?" His black eyes bored into hers.

Caroline shook her head slowly.

"No, I am here to teach the truth, and I'm here to learn the truth."

Crooked Feather's piercing eyes glared from under craggy eyebrows.

"I see you are no longer a Lost Child, Crooked Feather."

The black eyes slowly softened and the old familiar light ignited inside them. Crooked Feather smiled softly.

"Tell me, Caroline, did you decide which blood to follow? Did your life's story ever get back on the right path?"

She laughed lightly.

"I wish I knew for sure. But as my grandfather used to say, each story changes with the person telling it. If he was right, then I am sure that soon my life will become a beautiful story with a wonderful ending."

"Welcome home," Crooked Feather said. He smiled and gave the sign of friendship.